The X Variable

Madison Jackson

This book is dedicated to Juan, Ruben and Milly, who gave me hope that there are people in this world kind enough to let a thirteen year-old accomplish her dreams.

PROLOGUE

"Sir, I've got my sights locked on him," the man muttered into an earpiece in a low tone as he pushed through the crowd. He was tired but yet extremely alert as he made his way to the middle of the mass of people that never seemed to end. *I just want to go home,* he thought, although immediately after it was said he knew that he shouldn't have allowed himself to even think about it so soon. He had a bigger job to do, and he couldn't afford to screw it up.

The man of which everyone was gathered to see stepped onto the podium in front of the large crowd and silenced everyone. Even the faintest of whispers quieted down in order to hear the president speak, because that's who he was, and however important the low-level conversations might have been, no speech was more important than his.

A gust of wind swept over the thousands of people, ruffling hair and hats alike. Most of the people were all here to watch the president speak, of course, but the suited man in the midst of the gathering was there for an altogether different purpose.

He looked to his right, where another suited man wearing an earpiece caught his gaze and nodded before looking back to the president. This man was considerably older, and he was wearing sunglasses, although clouds blocked the sun's rays from reaching the people fully.

"Citizens of America," the man on the stage said as he leaned onto the podium. Two heavily muscled guards came up into his background, hopefully scaring away anybody who thought of harming the important man on the stage. The man in the crowd only smiled; he knew that, in almost every way possible, they were as harmful and dangerous as a child's teddy bear compared to him. In a way, though, the guards knew that too, and they were afraid of it. But the man pushed that out of his thoughts; he had to focus on the large crowd of people and the possibility that somebody might be there to do some major damage.

"I'm overjoyed to be here today. I've flown all the way from Washington to come here, and I'm glad I did!" After he said it, an explosion of applause and yelling swept over the guards, president, and everyone else. The man was cool, his eyes never leaving the president. "As you all know, I've come to address the issue of the Korean city-states and the attacks they've placed on us. Fear not, we have it under control, I can rightfully assure you. Remember, we may not be the largest country, but we are the most technologically advanced! After all, it is 2098, the year of the century!" Another, louder, roar erupted from the crowd, and still the man was as cool as he was before the president started his speech. He was not here to cheer or admire the president; far from it, actually. He was there to protect the speaker, and that was what he intended to do.

Although his eyes were on the president, his mind was focused on the people around him. To his immediate right, aside from his partner a few people to his left, a woman in a small, lacey, pink dress stood anxiously watching the president speak. To his immediate left, a man in a light blue shirt and dark blue jean-shorts stood with a giant grin on his face and a fist pumped into the air.

The man always enjoyed watching Americans' patriotism when the president spoke, although he himself had considerably less. In his mind, people had enough to cover for him; after all, he worked for the government. He didn't need patriotism, or that was at least how he viewed it.

Suddenly, a large, muscular man came up from behind him and moved to the spot just behind his right shoulder and beside the girl in the lace dress. In the process, he clipped his shoulder with the man's, who, annoyed, sharply glanced at him.

"Oops, sorry," the large man said. The other just smiled slightly and nodded once, returning his attention to the president.

Even after an hour of speech, the president did not falter once, and the crowd did not cease their endless enthusiasm. Every time the loyal president said something positive, the crowd blasted into the noise again, eventually leveling out the man's abnormally-long temper. A headache began to dawn inside of his head, causing him to focus on the president more so than the crowd. That is the reason he didn't see the man on his right come up close behind him and put a hand to his neck. Once the man noticed, which was almost immediately after, it was already too late. The needle was injected into a vein in his neck, and instantly his knees crumbled. His vision blurred, and his last sight was of the president before he blacked out.

1

Thump, thump. Thump, thump. The beat of his heart and his steady breathing was all he could hear as he flicked his eyes open. At first he saw nothing as his eyes squinted as they tried to adjust to the bright light. After he had taken a few seconds to get situated, he glimpsed around and saw that he was in a room; he looked down, and he noticed that he was on a small cot, in the middle of the bare, large room with grey walls and no windows. He also observed that he was dressed in faded jeans and a grey tank top that highlighted his muscular frame. Had he always been built like this? He couldn't remember; it hurt to think. At closer, painful, yet necessary observation, he noticed his height; he was taller than he imagined he would be, in the few short seconds he had to muse over his physical abilities, yet he had a faint feeling that he towered over everyone and *everything*. Actually, who WAS everyone, and what WAS everything? Now that he thought about it, who was HE?

The patient hurtfully thought and thought about his identity. No memories surfaced. No family, no house, no friends, nothing. The only memory he had were simple things, such as how to move and breathe. Though, somehow he had an eerie feeling about the room. He felt like he'd been there before. The faint memory haunted him until he urged himself to sit up to get a better view.

The blood from his head surged downwards, almost knocking him over. He had to lay down again for close to five minutes before he could properly think again. Once he managed to get his thoughts going, exiting through the door seemed inevitable. It was as though the door held all of the much-needed answers to the questions that flew through his mind.

The patient painfully sprang himself up, took a few practice steps, and lumbered towards the door. Even before he reached for the handle, he knew in his gut the door would be locked. Panic sprang through him. *What can I do now?* But then, as if on cue, he remembered. Somehow, as if by some holy omen, he recognized this lock. He seemed to know everything about it: the brand, the maker, and how to upspring the mechanism locking him inside the room. It was as though someone had specifically trained him for this very moment. So, in a matter of minutes, he had used a part of the belt he was dressed in to unhitch the lock, and it clicked in success.

He gripped the cold, steel handle of the door and held it in a firm grasp. If his method did not work, he had no reserve option. None at all, not in the slightest bit. He gave a silent prayer to anybody listening as he threw the door open. After he did so, however, he went temporarily blind and deaf as sirens blew at his eardrums and flashing red sirens pounded at his eyes.

At first he stood there, shocked, with his eyes squinting to fathom the painful new sensations, but then he went into action. The patient quickly surveyed the hallway, because going back was not an option. To his immediate right were two large, steel doors with handles of steel that he knew were locked. A keypad sat on a wall directly beside the doors. Going left wasn't an option; he heard rapidly approaching footsteps. Footsteps meant guards, which also mean weapons of some kind. That was something he didn't want to deal with. *What can I do?* He nervously thought about his situation. Instead of letting him continue on worrying, a voice came booming over the intercom, one that said something he would never forget.

2

The voice was deep and husky, and the patient knew he'd heard it before. "Don't fight. There's no use." Those were the first words the patient had heard since he'd awaken.

He looked up at the intercom and smirked. He was somehow very used to these threats, and yet he was also very accustomed to handling them on his own. He knew the intercom voice wasn't there to help him, and the footsteps approached faster with each ticking second. The doors to his right weren't options, and neither was going left to the seven approaching guards. *Wait,* he thought. *Seven guards? How can I know how many guards were coming?*

Deciding to put it off until later, the patient looked back up at the intercom, as if asking for answers. It was on a bare tiled ceiling, with the white audio propeller strangely out of place on the tan roof. Something beside it caught his hawk-like vision. It gave off the appearance of the same tan color, but anybody taking a closer look would see it was the slightest shade lighter, and had small, almost microscopic slits in it running the whole length of the tile. It reminded him somewhat of an air vent. He listened, trying to figure out what it was. An almost silent hum emanated from it, giving away its secret. It was an air vent, and possibly his way out. There was only one problem; it was on the ceiling, eight feet off of the ground.

The patient threw up his long arms, reaching desperately for the vent. He swore under his breath when he realized he was still six inches shorter than the ceiling.

The cot, a voice in the back of his head told him quietly. *Go back and get the cot!* He thought about it, but then realized that it was a decent idea. *Of course,* the patient thought. The cot in the gray room, the cot that started his only memory, his way to survival!

He raced into the room, and darted over to the cot. It looked foldable, like most cots were. The patient quickly folded the long legs in, and threw it against the floor, front first. He picked it up and repeated the same motion. *Just in case,* he thought. He hauled it up once more and barreled into the hallway, and then under the vent.

Within seconds he had the cot back on its legs, right beneath the vent. The patient sprung onto the silky under sheets and grasped the air vent holdings. He carefully lifted the ceiling tile. Now he couldn't be sure how far away the footsteps were, but they sounded dangerously close. He tore the tile away, revealing an air duct, just as he'd hoped. It looked just big enough for him to limber through. The patient hauled himself into it, laying on his elbows, and kicked away the cot beneath him.

His muscles burned with anticipation, and it was clear they hadn't been used to this degree in a long time. With the vent tile in one hand, he carefully and quietly put the tile back into place, securing his hiding place.

Now he was in a tight spot, literally. In order to fit

in the vent, he had to lie down on his stomach, and it wasn't comfortable at all. His breathing was restrained, and his actions limited.

Well, now I've no reserve-, his thoughts were interrupted by seven guards suited in blue uniforms surging around the corner and right under him. Six of them rushed into his room and started scouring the place inch by inch. One of them stood guard in the hall gazing at the cot, which was now up against the metal doors. The guard was young, maybe mid-twenties. *Twenty-six years old,* the voice in his head said. Weighing in at 125 pounds, the guard seemed fit and was holstering a handgun, but how long would that be the case? How long would it actually be *in* his holster? How did the patient actually *know* all of this?

"What is it doing over here?" the guard murmured. The runaway patient could see thoroughly through the slits of the vent.

"Hey, guys, did you even notice this?" the guard below him shouted to his comrades.

A bigger guard, the only one wearing a gun strapped across his back, came into view. He looked to be 250 pounds approximately, and didn't look like the type that liked to be given bad news. He examined the cot, a ticking time bomb waiting to go off. After a few dreadful minutes, which meant hours to the patient in the freezing air duct, the assumed commanding guard made his conclusion.

"He must've used it to try and ram the doors," he muttered to the other guard. He went up to inspect the front of the cot where the guard ran his burly hand over the front metal bar.

"I was right, the front bar is bent in numerous spots. The only problem is, these doors won't, wouldn't, budge without the key code. So, that means only one thing...," the guard trailed off, a solemn look crossing over his already grim face. "Oh no! Oh no, no, no, no, no. There's no way!"

"What is it, boss?" the smaller guard inquired, his eyes narrowing.

The commander slowly looked over at his under-positioned peer before stating his idea in a solemn tone. "It means he remembers."

3

I remember. I remember. I remember. Those were the words that irritated the patient beyond means. The problem, as it seemed, was that he in fact did NOT remember, especially not about anything involving them or himself. Although he could remember the simple things, it was as if somebody had gone in and played with his brain, toyed with it until he remembered nothing of use. Almost as if that was by design.

Breathe in, breathe out. It was all the same to him. It came naturally, as did walking, observing, his eyes picking up every movement and detail of anything and everything. He knew something was missing, he just couldn't place what it was.

The gentle in and out of the air through the vent gave him little cover, but little was enough. The guards below suspected nothing about the person right above their heads.

The patient knew he should be nervous, but he wasn't; he was in the largest sense calm. It was an odd sensation, to be calm in a nerve wracking situation, but he had somehow grown accustomed to it.

"He must remember. Otherwise he couldn't have guessed that code. It's impossible," the head guard mused more so to himself then to anybody else. Another guard seemed to hear it, though, and turned to his captain.

"Shouldn't we be going after him, if he did get through? If there is the slightest possibility he got out, he must remember, so he is a major threat to anybody he encounters. And you know as well as I do, he won't be too pleased with anybody in this building after what we've done to him."

The captain, who remained at the front of the cot became still. "Don't you think I know that? Now, tell me something. Where exactly would he go if he DID manage to escape? We're HUNDREDS of miles away from the nearest actual city!" he spat out, his voice growing stronger with every word.

The general then went over to the wall where the keypad was located and flipped up the cover. He then started in typing the key code.

"One oh one nine--," the patient murmured lightly while mimicking the key code to himself, and then instantly regretted it.

"Guys, did you just hear that?" a young, unsure guard asked. Suddenly, every one became still, even the patient's own breathing ceased.

"I must've been, uh, imagining things, sir," the suddenly frightened guard stuttered as soon as he realized that nobody else heard the sound. He looked to his commander waiting for the unavoidable command to leave, in a way, an inevitable death sentence. He stood there, waiting. The commander knew what he was thinking, because he was thinking the same.

"Don't be stupid. Come over here!" the commander shouted trenchantly. He was formidable in his choice of words.

The young, shaking guard hesitated, only making it worse for himself.

"I said come HERE!" the booming voice once again said. The sound traveled and echoed throughout the long, seemingly endless halls.

The patient could now clearly read the nametag the young guard wore, and it read "Agent Simon Parker, M5, 2098." *Is that the year?* He didn't know, it seemed ages before he had got out of that room, and now he had absolutely no memory of any year. For all he knew or remembered, it could have been year one.

Simon Parker slowly and carefully approached his general, afraid of the next movement. The remaining guards all kept their eyes on Parker, then the general, now back to Parker. None of them spoke up to save the young guard from his trouble.

"P-p-please, sir, I thought I heard something. I swear, sir," Parker pleaded. He now stood at the opposite end of the cot as the captain and was shaking as well. He latched his hand onto the steel bar of the cot, as if it was his lifeline now helping him stand.

The captain took a slow and lumbering step towards the young soldier. He raised back his hand by his head and brought it down with amazing force. The younger guard flinched, but it was not enough. The blow connected with Parker's left cheekbone, and he collapsed to the floor, banging his head on the cot on the way down. He lay still on the ground in a crumpled heap. Crippled and motionless lay the guard that once not so long ago sprang with energy and movement. Xavier closed his eyes in pity for the young Parker.

"Anybody else hear anything?" the old guard's voice rasped. He looked at the younger guards. A myriad of no's and no sir's went around to the patient's ears.

"Good. Now I need three of you to call for back up and secure the premises. The other two, grab him," he gestured to Parker, "and take him to Monroe." Nobody said anything about Parker after that as they drug him away by his front two limbs.

"I'll meet up with you guys at 16:00 hours at the

Bunk. Now, go!" The remaining guards shuffled off.

The captain stepped to the end of the cot and took a long look around. "I know you're listening, X. You remember. I don't know how, but you do. If you are interested in the deal we made before, meet me at the Caplar in one hour. You know where that is." With that, he typed in the key code 10195 and strode through the open doors.

The patient wondered about what he had just witnessed as he peered out between the small slits of the vent. He could just hear the fading footsteps when he realized he needed to move. It was quite dusty up there, even though he hadn't noticed it before. Now, however, he realized he had two choices: keep crawling and risk the chance that it would lead nowhere or jump down onto the floor, and try his luck at avoiding all other guards. Neither option sounded safe, he had to be honest with himself. Then again, he could handle unsafe. He felt capable that he could, memory or not.

With a sudden burst of courage, not worrying about what dangers lay ahead, the patient with no identity crawled into the bleak darkness ahead of him.

4

Anyone looking up at the vent would have never thought that the lost captive was up above, struggling for life.

Two loud, deep coughs echoed in the long and winding vents. He had crawled for what felt like hours, and his throat and lungs ached for clean air, which had stopped circulating a long time ago. The bull in him needed to keep going, but his heart and brain told him to give up and rest. It was clear these air vents hadn't been in use for ages; it seemed as though they just got dustier as he went along.

Maybe this building is old, he pondered. Older than himself, perhaps. Then again, he could be fifty and not know it, right? *No, actually, I can't. I can't be older than thirty, not with my muscles working the way they are.*

One thing was for certain; the patient desperately needed fresh air, which meant getting out of the deathly vent. It seemed never ending, even though he had come across one turn. He had barely been able to navigate through or around it. What he needed was a vent opening, like the one he'd entered through. That was his only hope of getting out of the metal prison.

~1 Hour Later~

He was hallucinating, he had to be! The patient could swear he saw light ahead, or maybe it was a mirage, he couldn't tell. It was only twenty feet away now. He was almost certain he could taste fresh air, smell it.

It was only five feet away. He knew now that it was a vent, finally! He had to desperately be quiet for the fear of somebody looking up and seeing him. He crawled up to it, slowly and stealthily. He peered downwards thorough the slits, déjà vu. The room was about ten feet wide on two sides and seven feet on the others, and maybe it was twelve feet tall, a cliff-diving jump. It was small and uninhabited by anybody that he could see. The bathroom looking room had a sink, lamp table no more than a few feet tall, with a lamp on it, and a toilet. *A bathroom for sure,* he thought. Somehow, however, almost conveniently, the table couldn't have been less than eight feet lower than the vent, which he was sure he could drop from if he need be.

He was no longer in need of air. For some reason, the vent had come back on about a half an hour ago. It felt heavenly, he couldn't lie to himself...*like being in a wind tunnel,* he thought.

Slowly and carefully, he dug his rugged fingers

under the tile and lifted up. He placed the tile on the reverse side of the hole the absent vent created. *Well,* he thought, *here goes nothing.*

It was a challenge getting down, even harder than it had been getting up. He had to go down feet first, there was absolutely no doubt about that. In order to do that, he had to crawl straight and straddle his stomach across the opening and dip his feet into the room and above the table. The patient couldn't knock the lamp over, surely somebody would hear it. So much pressure rested on his every single movement.

He dropped his feet into the opening and slowly lowered them. He was only about a microscopic inch away from the table. He supported all of his weight on his elbows as he lowered himself down that final inch until he was on the table.

He glanced at the door, hoping for some kind of locking mechanism that he could probably pick if he had to, in the event that it was locked. Fortunately, there was a deadbolt lock that would have to suit the situation. The patient quietly hopped down from the table on his toes and turned the lock. He had come this far and wasn't about to get trapped in a bathroom at the last minute.

Now what? He turned when movement on the wall

caught his eye. He braced himself in case the door opened, which was crazy, because nobody knew he was in there and the door was still locked. However, he looked, and what he saw gave him a new perspective.

What he saw was obviously a mirror, he knew that. It was his reflection that shocked him. A tall, ragged figure stared back at him. A character with bright blue eyes that went along perfectly with his shaggy yet trimmed black hair. He was steadily tanned and built like a football player. The patient showed his teeth, and the perfectly white and straight teeth shown back at him like stars. He had a perfect body, but he knew that probably didn't come without effort. His face was made up of his perfectly crafted teeth and lips, his dazzling eyes, and cheekbones fit for a model. Maybe he had been one in the past, but what did it matter now? It didn't, not unless he could smolder the guards to death.

Wow! Why am I so tall? Nobody is this tall, he told himself. The patient looked at his shoes, and those didn't help with the height issue. The new looking sneakers fit him exactly and gave him no more than one inch of height. His attention drew to the mirror again. On his neck were two markings that overlapped themselves. He lightly ran his fingers over them, tracing the figure. Moments later, he realized what he was touching was a tattered "X" tattooed onto his body.

He wondered what the letter could mean. The perfectly crafted patient couldn't think of anything, besides the fact that he now had a name.

5

X's eyes scanned over his body, looking for any other clues. Nothing. There was nothing on his arms, legs, or hands. Nothing. He did, however, find that he in no sense lacked in muscle, which clung to almost every single bone in his body.

He had large arms fit for a boxer and legs that could belong to an Olympic runner. He couldn't dwell on his new addition to his childlike memory, though, he decided. There were more important things, like what he was going to do. In fact, what was he going to do now? The vents were certainly not an option. He couldn't go back to those death traps. The hallway on the other side of the door was his only option. That was, if somebody didn't find him. He would have to take care of anyone who saw him in the open. He didn't know if the guards had alerted the people in the building or not. Or if there were even other people in the building. *Of course there are. Why would it only be me and a few banal guards?*

The patient had decided. He put his trained ear up

to the door and listened. Nothing but the quiet circulation of air rose to his ears, but he knew that was only the tip of the iceberg. There could be cameras, unlike the hallway he had recently come out of. *On second thought, why didn't they have cameras if they needed to keep me in? Something doesn't add up,* he thought, although he was already suspicious.

Deciding to take a chance, he soundlessly unlocked the door and put his quavering hand onto the knob. He could probably take on three or four guards if he had to, but if anymore than that came…

He didn't want to dwell too much on that thought. X slowly opened the door a crack, waited, and then opened it some more. Nothing happened, so he opened it halfway and stuck his head out.

To his right about twenty feet down was a right turn that led who knows where, and to his left was a long stretch of hallway with a left turn protruding from it about forty feet away. It was a big building, or at least from what he could see it was. He anxiously glanced at the ceiling for any cameras. There was none, as far as he could tell, but he knew he still had to be cautious.

Thump, thump, thump, thump. He could hear his heart racing, and he knew that wasn't normal. Should he be able to clearly hear his heart beat like he could hear the approaching footsteps? *Wait, what? Approaching footsteps?* Back into the bathroom he retreated. The footsteps came within feet of his room, and the patient decided to spring into action.

He threw the door open, almost breaking it at the hinges. The unsuspecting victim was harshly grabbed by the shoulders and thrown into the bathroom with X. The patient slammed the door shut and shoved the person dressed like a guard against the door, pinning him by his shoulders.

He needed answers, and who other to ask then a scared guard at the mercy of a runaway, if that's what he could be called?

"What do you know about the patient, the one with the X tattoo?" he yelled at the person, who he knew he had seen before. He was so familiar…that guard! What was it…Parker! Simon Parker, M5 2098! "Parker…," he whispered, something tugging at his memory.

What was once a scared look on the guard's face now spread to a smile of joy as big as the desert they were in. "X! It's you, and you remember me! Whew," he took time to lift his lower right arm and wipe imaginary or real sweat off of his brow. "That's a relief. Well to me I guess." Before he knew it, X had his hands swept away and was being drawn into a big hug.

"Get. OFF. Of. ME!" he yelled while pushing Parker away.

"No, what are you doing? It's me, your best friend! Don't you remember? Well I was told you remembered everything, so I said "Hey-"

"Stop talking!" X shouted. "Look, I don't have a 'best friend', and I have no idea who you are except that you are the young wimp of a boy that got beat up by a guard in the hallway!" Out of anger X shoved his arms directly beside Parker's temples on the wall. He looked at his face, which was directly across from his. Shock registered across the young guard's face, and X lowered his arms and stepped back.

"B-b-but you escaped. You remembered the password, you-wait." A confused look now took over Parker's face. "Wait, how did you see me black out?" Suspicion rose in his soft voice. "How?" he whispered. "Its impossible, you weren't there," he gave himself a humorless, reassuring laugh. "But, you, how?" His voice now was barely worthy of being called a whisper.

The patient couldn't come up with an answer that didn't give away his hiding place. He couldn't trust anyone, especially a young guard. Could he?

No, he thought. He couldn't trust anyone,

especially a guard. *That is his number one priority, or at least it should be,* he thought honestly.

"I'm not going with you, because I know you'll want me to. Turn me in, if those are the right words. I don't know what they'll do to me, and I don't want to know. So why don't you do exactly as I say and waltz out of here like nothing ever happened? You can go along, say you caught a glance of me if you have to. Just say nothing of this. Understand?" he commanded in a fierce voice.

The young guard smiled and shook his head, a confusing action for X. "X, you always were hard headed. Guess that didn't change," Parker replied, as if they had been best friends for the longest of times. "I wouldn't expect it to, though. So, what's our plan now?" he asked.

As if X couldn't become more confused, he was now. "Wait, now. There is no us, we, or our. Got it? Just me, myself, and I. So go on, leave now before you get yourself hurt."

The guard looked down at the ground, then back up. "You know, I don't think I can do that." Now X prepared for the worse.

"And why is that?"

An elegant smile highlighted Parker's green eyes, making X want to wipe it off of his face all the more. "You don't think I'd leave my best friend, do you?"

6

"Well, what do we do now?" Parker asked X while perched on the lamp table. They had been in the bathroom for more than an hour now. After constant bugging, X was finally annoyed enough to tell him how he managed to get in the bathroom, and Parker listened intently. He hadn't said anything, interrupted, or even shook his head until his story was finished.

"Wow, buddy, you haven't lost it, have you? My god, you're a freak," he had said with a disbelieving laugh. Parker knew X couldn't believe it himself, so he let it go after a while. The young guard then went on to tell his story.

"Well, I came here a few months after we met Monroe, remember?" X shook his head and looked at the floor. "Oh. Right, you don't remember. I don't really know much about what they did to you. I mean, I was told barely anything. They told me 'follow orders, stick to them, and don't ask questions.' That's the thing, I didn't ask questions. I hadn't even thought about it. Until they brought you in. I was standing guard beside the Operation Room that day. That's the room where they do all of their 'special' operations, among other things. It's weird. People come in, but they don't, well…leave. Well, they don't leave very often," he paused to glance at the still locked door.

"You were being carried, or should I say dragged in by your arms. Our two biggest guards had you, Anthony and Saul. You were kicking and fighting so hard, it was unbelievable. Obviously, you had left your mark on them, as they had on you. I ran to help you, but I didn't know who you were, and the next thing I knew, I was being dragged backwards by another guard! Oh, it was terrible. They kept me in a holding room for uncountable hours until I got myself straightened out. I worried for the longest of times, and then I had to assume the worse when I didn't hear from you. They let me out, and they told me we had a new project, X was his name. I thought maybe it was you. You know? X for Xavier? Then when Monroe told me I was his friend, well that erased all doubts in my mind at the-,"

"Wait," the patient said. "Xavier. That's my name?" he looked up at Parker hopefully.

"Yeah, it is," came Parker in response.

Xavier let out a sigh of relief. "Huh. Who would've thought. I have a name. Okay. I have a name."

"Yes, congrats, buddy. Nice to know that you know what your own name is."

After a few moments, Xavier spoke up again. "Well, what do we do now? Don't you think we should focus on getting me out of here? It's not exactly a walk in the park, waltzing me out of here. Based on what you've told me, it seems that they have pretty firm sights set on me." He took a seat on the sink edge.

Parker thought on this for a second. He seemed deep in thought when the door handle moved. It was followed by two loud thuds on the door.

"Hey, is anyone in there?" a deep voice rang through. It was rough, like the one Xavier imagined a bull would have if it could talk. Both the patient and the guard recognized that voice, and it wasn't pleasant. Parker's face sank in disbelief. His eyes spread wide, and he gave Xavier a gut sinking look.

"Look," he voiced in a whisper. "That's Anthony, the guard who almost killed me. We have to be quiet, but I have a plan." He raised his voice up so the guard outside could hear him. "Hey, yeah Anth. It's just me, Simon. I'll be out in a second." A grunt came from outside the door in response.

"Okay, here's the plan. No arguing. You're either in

or you're dead. Got it?"

A nod came from Xavier, who didn't believe in wasting time.

"We're going to go out there and hope he doesn't notice who you are. Stay on my left so he can't see you as well. Here, switch me shirts so he doesn't recognize your clothes. Hurry!" Parker commanded in a harsh whisper.

Xavier took off his shirt, revealing a tan and toned chest, once again making him think of the model deal. "Parker, I know this isn't the time, but was I a model before I came here?" he asked quickly while pulling over Parker's shirt. An odd and disbelieving look came from Parker to X.

"You're right. Now is NOT the time!" he yelled quietly at the patient.

A hurried series of nods came from Xavier, marking that he was ready to take action and stop goofing off.

Parker leaped down from his lamp table perch and soundlessly unlocked the door. It clicked with satisfaction as he twisted the knob with ease. Xavier got down while planting his feet firmly as he stood to

Parker's left.

Letting out a sigh, Simon Parker swung open the door and strode out of the bathroom with the escaped patient on his direct left. They made an odd pair, but Xavier hoped it would work on the oldest guard.

Anthony's eyes swept over the pair quickly, and then found their way back to the patient. Suspicion rose, and then realization hit him. "You!" he yelled, but the runaway patient was already in motion.

The youngest guard swept back and let the patient do what came naturally to him. Xavier grabbed Anthony's arm easily and brought it around his back while pinning his face to the wall. It was all done in one fluid motion.

"Now, you'll give me your full cooperation before I let you go. Clear?" X demanded. He didn't know how he had gotten a hold of the guard so fast, so easily. All of it surprised him by the natural ease of it.

A menacing laugh escaped from the old guard, sending chills through Parker. He'd gone over to the bathroom door and opened it, waiting.

"I always knew you'd help him," he spat out at Parker. "Choosing that over us, how despicable. And you, Xavier, you didn't take up our deal. Tell us why. Why not take it? It sets up perfectly for you. Nobody would question you again."

This annoyed Xavier beyond meaning. Not just that, but the fact that he couldn't remember the deal, and now he was being questioned about it. Now he was beyond annoyed; he was vexed. Utter and unparalleled annoyance flowed through him.

He shoved the guard's head into the wall all the farther, making it the most uncomfortable and painful position for the guard as he could. "I had a change of plans. That's all you need to know." He gritted through his teeth as he spoke, "Now, tell me, which way is out?"

Anthony couldn't move his head, but he could barely move his body. He tried to move and escape X's painful hold, but it made the patient hold him all the tighter. "Isn't that something your friend Simon will tell you?" That same laugh rang again, but this time it did not hold defeat. Rather, it held a knowing sense of victory.

"No," Xavier said, almost to the point of breaking his neck and getting it done and over with. "I'm asking you. Now, left or right? Make it easy on yourself." As if his face couldn't become more compressed, X shoved it up against the wall so the guard could barely breathe.

He looked over at Parker for clearance, who was leaning nonchalantly against the wall. He nodded carelessly.

"I'll not tell you anything," the older guard said through his compressed face.

"Okay, we're clearly not getting anything out of him." Xavier muttered to himself. He put his mouth by Anthony's ear. "Now, be aware that I could in fact kill you in one roll of my fist. You know that, and I know that. Parker knows that as well. But I won't do that, because I'm not like you, even though it would satisfy me so much, and I wouldn't lose one blink of sleep. You have no idea who I am, and I intend to keep it that way. Now, when we go, you won't tell anybody of this. You know why? Because I will find you, hunt you down if that's what it takes, and kill you," he removed his head and looked at Parker, who was suppressing a laugh.

Xavier brought the guard back from the wall and slammed him into it again in one motion. He then let go of his elbow and turned Anthony towards him. The guard turned towards the other direction to run but was met by Xavier's upwards fist slamming into his chin, sending his head backwards. Parker had come up to catch Anthony's fall, making sure to cause no further unnecessary noise. Anthony's big body fell towards Parker with force. A look of knowing horror spread across Parker's face before he collapsed under the body.

"Ah, gross! Hey, you, help, *now*!" Parker yelled at Xavier, who was laughing hysterically at his friend.

"Come on, man, this isn't funny! This man has had one too many sweet cakes! Come help me!" He was centered between Anthony and the floor, which made it all the more humorous to X. His struggling added to the hilariousness factor.

After he was done laughing, Xavier went over to help his friend.

"Okay," he said as soon as they'd put Anthony in the bathroom and closed the door. "Left or right? You do know…," he hesitated before nervously laughing. "Right?"

Parker laughed a laugh full of humor. "We have to hurry. He won't be out long. Left."

7

The pair had scrambled off in the opposite direction of right. Xavier had prayed that no guards would find them, and so far they hadn't. Parker had taken them in a route that must be only used for important use, because it looked unused for a while. Upon being asked, the guard had only replied "they only use it for important matters, like you. Don't worry, nobody but me usually uses this hallway at this time anyway."

The patient had many questions. Oh, did he ever have questions. Many different inquiries zoomed through his mind at a rapid pace. *What year is it? How did I get mixed up in all of this? Why me? Who is Monroe?* So many of them raced past his brain, but he knew right now was not the time to ask them. He didn't want to risk anybody hearing them, although he assumed the building probably didn't carry sound very well.

"We have to take a left here, so turn." Parker said in a normal voice to the patient, confirming his thought about traveling sound in this building. The pair turned while walking side by side. If either of them were seen, at least the switch of shirts would help them. Xavier's gray shirt didn't go along with Parker's green trousers, but they didn't stand out so much as to cause suspicion among anybody passing by.

Catching a glimpse of the pair would only lead you to wonder about the fashion choice of the new guards. Although the pair didn't look totally out of place, Xavier didn't so much as look as Parker's twin. Xavier was six feet five inches when he walked, but Parker was only five feet eleven at the maximum. The young guard walked uncertainly while it was the patient who walked with purpose. He had a meaningful stride that could tell a lot about what he'd been through, Parker had said. After all, what HAD he been through? Xavier had asked that question, but the guard only replied with a doubtful you'll-find-out-soon-enough look. The patient hadn't exactly been satisfied with that, but he quickly learned that with Parker you couldn't interrogate any further than what he let off. Even though he tried interrogating more, he got interrupted abruptly.

"But you have to tell me. I have a right to know, at least give me that. What made them choose me out of-"

Parker stopped and turned towards the patient, who was still on his left. He held up a defenseless hand. "Buddy, I can't tell you any more. I know I've already sold my soul by helping you, trust me, this agency will kill me once they find out I helped you. But there are things even YOU shouldn't know quite yet, but when the time comes, I promise I'll tell you. Only if you stop asking. Deal?" Xavier had nodded in agreement.

"Good." Parker continued on walking, motioning for Xavier to hurry up and follow. They turned down another hall with a padlocked door about half way down. A door with two steel handles and a keypad waiting to have a code entered into it.

"Parker, this isn't, is it?" Xavier said in normal tone

to his the guard on his left, who had become shrouded in seriousness as soon as he started down the long hall. A quick nod of the head confirmed the patient's question. "Wow..." he muttered "So this is it. Can I see the room?" They arrived at the door, walking past the patient's old room, the place that started it all. There was no window, but Xavier could tell that it was closed to keep people out, not to trap the escapee.

Parker went up to the keypad and stopped. He seemed to consider the idea of letting his best friend go back to his old room, or at least the room his memory started in. He shook his head afterwards, reprimanding himself for at most considering it.

"No. It's time consuming, and not to mention they probably have cameras scouring every inch of that room now." He typed in the code for the door and they opened with a swoosh that demanded attention of all onlookers. That got the patient thinking. Not about the doors, but about the cameras.

"Hey Parker," he ran up to catch the guard. "Why don't you guys have cameras in the halls?" Simon halted to consider this.

"Well, we don't really need cameras. Okay, we didn't before you showed up. Now they might be a bit helpful for them to use in this certain situation!" He gave himself a reassuring laugh and continued walking. The hall looked the same as the other side, only it came to a stop twenty feet ahead, offering only a left or right turn. It took only a moment for Simon to decide to take the right path. They turned, and this time the hall didn't have a menacing left or right turn to make leading a ways down. At the end of the hall stood a handled door without a lock or keypad. The patient's imagination took off at the sight of this, wondering what was behind the door. It could be anything, and that's what haunted him.

"Okay, I know what you're about to ask so I'll answer it and save you the trouble. Behind that door up there is the Caplar, the base where we keep all of our planes and some of our most valuable vehicles. So I guess you could call it a hangar sort of thing. Now, we're going to go in there and hopefully manage to get a land rover." This got a disbelieving look from Xavier. "Yes, I know it will be hard, but I know where the keys are kept and I know the way out of this place. Just do everything I say when I say it and we should be good." He approached the door and pulled out a set of keys from his pocket that Xavier didn't know he had. He made a mental note to later ask what each separate key did.

Parker jammed one of the keys into the door and twisted it. It didn't move, resulting in him trying another one. This time, it fit. Parker twisted it and opened the door. He entered the room and Xavier followed.

They both entered what could barely be called a room. It was more like there was a steel dome encasing the sky. It looked as though you could fit anything in there, even a planet. The hangar was new to Xavier, making it all the more interesting. His eyes scoured the room, taking in every detail. There were three enormous planes, which looked to be cargo carriers, the kind in which the army took in avid use to carry cargo with. Then to the right of the monsters were eight polished cars like Xavier knew he had never seen before. They were cars, but at the same time they weren't. The vehicles had four large wheels and were no bigger than a regular SUV, but they had the shape of a dune buggy. No roofs were on them, just a metal cage surrounding the dual seats.

"Are you serious? We're taking these?" Xavier said while giving a laugh. He'd expected something a little less modern, but he knew then that he'd expected wrong. He walked up to one and scaled over it with his eyes. He was like a child in a candy shop. The patient had taken immediate interest in the vehicles, leading Parker to say something about it.

"You were a mechanic, before. Not for long, maybe a month or so. But you loved cars." He said it quietly so that Xavier could barely hear him. X turned around to face Parker, wanting more. He knew he couldn't ask for fear of annoying his now serious friend. If that happened, all of his information about his past life would be swept away. He settled to ask about their location instead.

"These are desert rovers." he said knowingly. "We must be in the desert, right? So what desert are we in?"

Parker got out yet another key from his pocket and hopped into one of the buggies, ignoring him. "Are you coming?" he yelled at Xavier in a happy tone. The patient lumbered over and swung himself into the vehicle.

"We're in the Sahel desert," Parker said. He took the key and jammed it into ignition. The engine roared to life with a dominance that would make any other engine cower. The purring of the engine made Xavier throw his head back and laugh.

"Haha!" Xavier laughed. "I'm in the Sahel desert in a buggy with a guard who works for people trying to kill me." He took a minute to let the realization sink in. As much as he had already been through in that day, and as much time as he had to think, he hadn't quite thought about what he'd done. He'd escaped a squad of guards, crawled through endless vents, jumped into a bathroom, gotten by one of the supposedly biggest guards the organization had to offer, and was going off into the Sahel desert in Africa in a dune buggy. All in one day, he hadn't done bad. But why hadn't they seen more guards from the organization controlling them?

Simon clearly isn't going to tell me anything about this place, he thought. *Especially not the name of it.* So what could he call it instead of the place that tried to hold him captive? This organization that kept him...the Org. The Organization. He decided that would have to fit for now. The Org was the place that started his new memory, and would hopefully never be in his mind again.

"Hey Parker, where are we going?" The guard shifted into reverse toward a door that took up the entire opposite wall with the door of the enormous cylinder. "We just can't barge through the wall...can we?" Xavier looked confused with the situation.

Simon threw down the gear and the buggy flew backwards. He reached his hand down towards where the radio on a normal car would be to a green button labeled 'Open'. The guard pushed the button in, and behind them the double doors stretching the height of the hangar opened up with a dramatic presence. Outside shined in and almost blinded the patient. A bright blue sky greeted him and he turned backwards in his seat and raced towards it while still in reverse.

After getting all the way out, Parker pressed a similar button, only this one was labeled 'Close'. *That's convenient,* Xavier thought. In response, the big hangar doors closed, marking off the exit of the escaped patient.

"How can you be sure nobody heard those open and close?" Xavier had a point. The doors made a sound so loud that somebody hearing it was inevitable.

"We can't," Parker said.

8

The pair had just gotten out of Caplar, and Parker threw the rover into drive. It lurched forward with a grateful roar and took off towards the endless hills of the Sahel. There were no direct paths, but Parker seemed to know his way.

"Where are we going?" Xavier once again asked. He knew that they couldn't drive on through the desert forever.

"There's a town twenty miles north of here!" Parker screamed over the gust of wind and sand coming through the spot where a windshield normally would be. "Get in that glove box and get out two pairs of goggles!"

Xavier looked down, and he saw a glove box that went previously unnoticed. He pulled out the lever and it sprang open. Inside it were three pairs of goggles that would work, a roll of duct tape, three pairs of gloves, and one pair of pliers. *An interesting combination,* he thought.

He grabbed two pairs of goggles and tossed one into the driver's lap. Parker gratefully grabbed them with one hand and put them one his face. Xavier did the same. Having the sand fly at their faces didn't help their escape, but the goggles aided them tremendously.

The sand flying at them pelted their faces, as did the wind. Xavier didn't know if he could put up with it for twenty miles, but he was hoping he could. He had to; if not, the Org. might find him, because they must already be on a full scale man hunt.

Xavier tried to imagine the whole team scouring every inch of ground to find him, only to realize he wasn't there anymore. Only to realize that Parker was gone, either taken captive or helping the patient. He didn't want to think about what would happen if they found his himself. Xavier knew that they wouldn't kill him, because if they wanted him dead he would be dead already, not just without memory. He must have been kept alive for something. But he made no promise about Parker. They would torture him, and then kill him once they got everything out of him. The thought made him shiver, sending a chill up his spine. It felt like he had just met the guard, but he had already come to care about his well being.

The patient had come to realize he had nothing to do to pass the time, so he took to looking at the dashboard of the vehicle. The speedometer showed them going fifty miles per hour, a slow speed for a dune buggy of this kind. It was extremely slow, granted, but it felt like 100 miles per hour with no roof or windshield.

He was deep in thought when it hit him. It came on fast, like a bullet. Blackness started spreading over his mind like clouds rolling over the smoky night horizon. At first he could see well, but then blackness was only half of what he could see. Xavier stole a glance at Parker to see if the same thing was happening to him, but he looked fine. Parker looked over at him, and he was immediately worried.

"Xavier? Xavier, talk to me! Come on, buddy talk to me!" His voice was slowly fading from Xavier's reality as he blacked out.

Xavier opened his eyes wearily. Light flashed, taking up all of his vision, but then it stopped. He blinked his eyes a few times, trying to figure out where he was and why he wasn't still in the desert.

Now Xavier was in a kitchen, one he thought he would see in a restaurant. He was standing behind a wall, staring at two people talking in the very back. His head peaked out from behind the wall, barely letting off his presence. His vision was perfectly clear, almost hawk-like. One of the people was wearing a dark blue suit with a black tie, and his hair was as black as the midnight sky. The other was wearing a gray suit, with a white tie, looking very suave. He gave off the sense of dominance, and the patient knew he knew that from somewhere. The pair were obviously in an argument, or a heated discussion, and the gray suited person seemed to be winning.

The kitchen was completely deserted, aside from the suited men and the patient. Xavier looked down at himself, and he himself was dressed in a black suit with a white dress shirt. He looked very professional himself, and he almost didn't recognize it. He had black dress pants on, and they fit comfortably, as did his suit.

"You know we can't do that. Monroe would have our heads if anybody found out we were even talking about this. He's killed enough, he wouldn't mind killing off two of his own," the gray suited person hurriedly whispered. He looked around the room to secure their conversation, making the patient retreat behind the wall. That was when he realized that he had no control over his movements. When his body jerked back, at the same time his body stayed there. It was almost like a dream. He took three steps back and realized his body didn't move at all, only his vision did. He had a full body, but nobody could see him.

"Hey!" he yelled at the people arguing while stepping out in full vision of them. They didn't move, or even notice him. They just continued on in their argument.

"But, for God's sakes, he's planning to kill Roger Clemons! Doesn't that mean anything to you? Our whole world, our whole country, would be thrown into chaos! All because of a personal grudge? Sorry, but I don't feel like going to jail for LIFE! We can't tell Monroe about our plan!" the blue suited person yelled as quiet as he could. This left a series of questions flowing through Xavier's mind. Who was this Roger Clemons, and why did Monroe want him dead? He came up beside the people to hear better.

Up close, the men exerted the presence of young age. The blue suited man could have been no older than twenty, a baby. Meanwhile, the gray suited man must have been no older than thirty, while being no younger than twenty. The young one had a handkerchief neatly tucked into his patch pocket of his suit that stated cleanly "Bryier." *That must be his name,* the patient mused.

"Come on! Why are you all of a sudden bailing on me? Wasn't it our plan from the beginning to take over what Monroe started? We'll just get together the other eight and then continue our plan! What's so dangerous about that?" Now the gray suited person was talking. This one didn't even have a pocket, let alone a handkerchief that sported his name.

"I told you, I'm not doing it! I'm not going to kill for power! Do you have any idea of how wrong that is? I know, I went with it before but I never actually thought you'd go along with it! I can't, I won't do it! No!"

The gray suited person nodded his head, like he expected this answer, but he simply refused to believe it. "Now, you listen up, and you listen well." He reached inside a pocket on his pants and pulled something out. After closer examination, Xavier realized it was a hand gun. Dangerous and stealthy, this man was not joking around. The man in the gray suit shoved the gun against Bryier's stomach, causing him to flinch. His eyes opened in surprise and released a knowing realization.

"You're going to help me kill Monroe. You know why? Because I'll kill you if you don't. Don't think I won't, because you know I will. You know perfectly fine I will. You'll go back out there, take your seat next to Monroe, and do exactly as I say. Clear?" The gray suited person who had once been the omega was now clearly the alpha in this conversation. Bryier nodded, and looked down at the ground in submission.

"Okay," he muttered unwillingly.

A quick burst of air came and smacked Xavier harshly across the face.

"Ouch!" he yelped in surprise. *What was that?* Now his vision was becoming fuzzy around the edges. Another quick swipe of air attacked the patient's face. *What IS that?* It left the patient wondering.

"Snap out of it!" a commanding voice blasted over his ears. It was like being in the hallway, with the voice coming out of the speakers. Only this time the voice was loud and commanding, not suggesting like the intercom's was. The pain in his head was unbearable, and it brought the patient to his knees. He sank to the floor, his hands on his ears. He tried to block out any sound from reaching his throbbing ears.

The two men turned in his direction, only it wasn't in his direction. It was the other Xavier's direction, his body of the memory. Xavier's face turned to action as he quickly darted around the corner away from the two men.

"Get him!" the gray suited man commanded Bryier,

who was already on his way to Xavier. Now the patient could barely see anything, let alone hear anything anymore. Another rush of air hit him across the cheek, and this time it connected hard. The blow knocked him over, leaving him writhing on his side on the floor. Suddenly everything became black, and Xavier wasn't aware of anything.

———

He woke up in the right seat of the dune buggy, with Parker continually slapping his face with massive force. "Ow. Ow," his voice kept getting louder. "OW! Cut it out, Parker!" Xavier yelled, with his eyes adjusting to the new, brighter light. "What was that for?!" he shouted with anger while his face dealt with the pain.

"What was that all about? Besides scaring me half to death? I thought you just died on me!" Parker shouted with anger. Another rush of air slapped across Xavier's face, and this time he realized it was always Parker's hand connecting with his face.

"OW! What was that one for?" Xavier exclaimed,

now angered.

Parker returned to facing the open desert and started driving again.

"That was because I thought you were dead! Now," Parker said, starting to cool down. "Are you going to tell me what that was all about?"

Xavier thought about this, his face still throbbing. "Well, I think I had a flashback of ***why*** and ***how*** I was taken."

9

"Well, do tell!" Parker said anxiously. He was trying to drive slow to create less sound for Xavier to talk. So far, it had worked quite well. It slowed their speed down from fifty miles per hour to thirty, but it was all the same to the patient. He needed to tell somebody about this, and the only person within miles to tell was Parker.

"I was in a kitchen, of a restaurant, I think. These two guys were fighting, one of them was a young kid named Bryier. Heard of him?" He looked over at Parker, who was shaking his head slowly. It was almost like he believed Xavier was telling him a lie.

"Nope, never heard of him. Maybe you misread it and saw Bryien? Did he have dark black hair?" Xavier nodded his head and Parker continued. "Yeah, he was one of my friends, one of the good ones. He wasn't a bad kid, really. Just hung out with bad people is all. He helped catch you in the end of the nineteen month long search for you. Power was on his mind, that was all he ever thought about after associating with Shannon." He paused to wait for Xavier's comments.

"Wait, did you say it took nineteen months to find *me?* Seriously? I'm impressed!" Xavier gave off a laugh, surprising Parker in the odd situation.

"Xav, you make it sound like its nothing! You've always been like that, you know? Everything's so easy for you. I used to envy it SO much, and I'm pretty sure I still do!"

Smiling, Xavier continued. "Okay, they were arguing. Something about killing Monroe to protect Robert Clemons. Who's that?"

"Woah, woah, woah, what? Killing Monroe? Who, Bryien and Shannon? No way! That little bug!" Parker exclaimed with force. He looked from Xavier to the wheel of the vehicle, and then to the endless desert encasing them like he couldn't believe what he was hearing.

"And to answer your question, Robert Clemons is the president, and he has been for three years. Monroe hates him, wants him dead, yeah you've gotten that. But what I didn't know was that Bryien and Shannon are planning to kill Monroe for the sake of Clemons! For some reason I don't think that's going to go very well for them," he muttered, seemingly deep in thought.

Xavier was just focusing on trying to wrap his mind around all of this. Who were the Org. exactly, and was Monroe at the head of it? He had too many questions and not enough answers, so he decided to leave it alone for a while. The patient lay his head back on the head rest and shut off from the outside world for what moments he had.

Eventually, the faint outline of some buildings came into view. They weren't tall, they looked like shacks. Maybe this was the town Parker had talked about: It seemed as though they had driven more than twenty miles, perhaps thirty. Xavier had lost track after his flashback, if it could be called that. They had started going faster and faster, working their way back up to fifty miles per hour or above as they got closer and closer.

"Hey Parker, is that the town you were talking about?" he yelled over the gushes of wind pounding at them as they drove.

Parker yelled something inaudible as he flew over a hill. The dune buggy went airborne for a moment before it hit the ground with a thud. Xavier jerked forward, almost flying out the front of the vehicle.

"Okay, slow it down Parker! We're not racing anybody!" Xavier yelled at his companion, who was speeding off with his foot to the floor on the accelerator. "I mean it, Parker, slow down before you kill both of us!" This seemed to get to Parker, because he slowly lifted his foot off of the floor, but he didn't slow down by much.

"Sorry, I didn't hear you. I'm just so nervous, we've got to get there!" He stole a glance at Xavier, who was hanging onto one of the bars of the cage as if it were his lifeline. At seeing this, Parker threw back his head in a laugh.

"You're SO not made for desert life!" he yelled at Xavier. In return, the patient threw him an annoyed look.

Xavier finally got Parker to slow down when they reached the village. There was only one main street going through the middle of the town, and the huts surrounded the road. It wasn't paved, and the sand still flicked itself at the pair. *It is only dirt,* Xavier kept telling himself. *It can't hurt that badly.*

The huts looked old, and they were definitely damaged by the harsh desert winds. At the opposite edge of town Xavier could see a few trees, maybe palm trees, he wasn't sure. The town had few people walking along side their houses, and most of them were carrying baskets with some kind of object in them.

Parker slowed down even more and they drove on the road through the village. It seemed as though everybody stopped what they were doing and stared at the vehicle. It was eerily silent, but Xavier didn't know why. Perhaps the people weren't used to vehicles. Or soldiers. *Do they know about the Org. just 20 miles away? Have they been in contact?* So many questions took over the patient's mind that he decided he needed a log to keep them all in.

He felt so out of place in the small village. Xavier knew Parker felt the same way. He looked over at the guard, and he had a face covered by seriousness. Parker was staring straight ahead, seeming to be looking at something. Xavier followed his gaze and saw the only actual building in the village.

"Hey Parker, what's that up there?" Xavier asked, referring to the actual building. He could see it better after a few seconds since the sun wasn't directly in his gaze. It was a single story building, and it wasn't big, either. It looked like a doctor's office, one you would see in a small town. The outside walls were painted gray, and it had windows on about every side. A pair of glass doors marked the entrance, making it less menacing. It could have been no smaller than the size of fifteen huts, easily, too.

"This, is the home of the one person that can help you," Parker replied.

Parker pulled up to the edge of the street parallel to the building. "Get out," he said as he turned the key left, shutting off the dune buggy. "And hurry up, too." The guard went around the side of the vehicle and strode off to the doors. Xavier swung himself out of the buggy and followed behind him.

"Ladies first." Simon opened the door, motioning for Xavier to enter first. Xavier rolled his eyes at his friend, who seemed to be unworried. Then he entered with Parker right behind him. The young guard seemed to be back to his worry free self, which relaxed Xavier. Although he wasn't relaxed, it helped him that Parker, the only person he knew, was.

Inside was like a oasis inside a desert, metaphorically and literally. Right in front of them was an inside waterfall cascading from the ceiling that pooled into a pond at the bottom. On either sides of it were long, leather couches that emanated money and pride in the room. The floor was tiled neatly, and the walls were lavished with pictures of people that Xavier didn't know.

On one of the couches sat a suited man deeply into a newspaper. Parker coughed, letting him know of their presence. The man lowered his newspaper and looked up at the pair.

"Ah, Simon! What brings you here today?" He took a look out of the corner of his eye at Xavier. "Oh my God."

10

Xavier walked in, unsure of this person.

"Nico, this Xavier. Xavier, this is Nicolas Hedge." Parker said, gesturing to the man lounging on the couch. Nicolas Hedge's eyes swept over the patient, seeming to remember his exact movement. After moments of this, finally Nicolas spoke.

"Please, Nicolas Hedge was my father. I'm Nico. Only in business am I Nicolas Hedge." He said it to Xavier, who was taking in all the information. Nico had a certain coolness that he exerted into the room around him. He seemed to know he was in control, the one who called all of the shots, even though he didn't seem to care.

"We're here because I need your help," Parker said. He looked over at Xavier helplessly. "I'm-" he stopped to correct himself. "We're here because we need your help. This is X." The guard said, and that seemed to seal the deal. Nico's eyes lit up at this, and his face filled up with joy.

"Of course, I'm no fool!" Nico proclaimed with newfound excitement. "I've heard legions about you since, well, you know. It's a pleasure, really, to finally see you again!" The man leapt up and extended his hand to Xavier, who shook it skeptically. *What does this man mean by 'again'?*

"Excuse me, but what exactly have you heard about me, and from who?" Xavier asked. He wasn't too sure about who this man was, and whether Parker trusted him fully or not. *Then again,* he thought, *Parker may be the person who told Nico all about my memory loss.*

"Simon, why don't you go settle yourself in your room while I explain things to Xavier here?" he suggested to Parker, who obliged almost unwillingly. Nico gestured to a hidden door to the far right of the room, where an unnoticed before kitchen and door stood. Parker went over and opened the door and went into it, almost like he'd done this before.

"Take a seat, and I'll answer all of your questions to the best of my ability. Sound good?" Nico asked the patient, who nodded succinctly. They went over and sat on the couch nearest to the right of the waterfall, which was gushing down right next to them. Xavier felt uncomfortable in a room all alone with somebody he didn't truly know, who could very well have a weapon anywhere they so desired. But Parker trusted Nico, which was Xavier's only regain of confidence. He sat on the opposite end as the man, though, just to be safe.

"I knew you before, which is how I know everything about you. Your dad and I were the best of friends; we are actually brothers. So I guess you could say I'm your uncle. Sound okay so far?" he asked, while looking at the dazed patient.

Thoughts raced through his head. *Family, real family! Okay, I may not remember him, but still! Somebody I knew besides Parker!*

"Okay..." he muttered. "Sounds good. Continue on, if you must." Xavier was trying hard not to show how anxious he was to hear more answers to his never-ending questions, but that anxiety was slowly slipping through in his tone of voice.

Taking a deep breath like he expected to talk for a long period of time, Nico sighed. He looked content, but not angered or annoyed like Xavier would've imagined somebody related to him to look like when they were explaining anything. Not that he had pictured his family, though.

"All I know is that when I went away on vacation, I didn't hear from either of you two for a long time. I didn't know what was up, and I didn't really care. I mean, my nephew and brother are strong, right? What could possibly happen to them? Well I got home and then you two were just gone without a trace. Nobody had heard from you two, not even Simon. I had assume that you two were taken by them, because of, you know." He paused, seeming to remember something. "Never mind. Give me some time to wrap my mind around this. Believe me, there are so many rumors circulating about where you just came from around here, it's actually kind of funny. Some people say it's an agency to train soldiers, some say its a base built to assemble nuclear missiles. Of course I know the truth, because of Simon there."

As if on cue, the young Parker stepped out of his room and came over by the two men. He stood above the couch for a second, but then decided pulling a stool up from the kitchen bar was much better than sitting in between them.

"Nico, Xavier was wondering about his past. Will you save me the trouble?" The young guard asked. Nicolas gave Simon a *gee, thanks* look, but then started on.

"Well, from what I know, you were born in 2076, on February 9. Your mother was Angelica Hider and was married to your father, who was Joseph Hider. He was a worker for the CPAA before quitting to help raise you. Angelica was a social worker, she helped find homes for lost orphans around your town. She was a much loved face in her community, rest assured. Oh, yeah, you guys used to live in a town called Independence, in the old California. That of course was before the combination of Nevada, California, and Oregon into one territory." He looked to Parker, leaving his statement open for him to add anything. Parker shook his head, and motioned for him to continue on with his documentary.

"Oh, before I go on, let me explain to you what the CPAA is. It stands for the Critical Protection Agency of America, and it was founded in 2032 to help protect our country from any major threats. Somewhat like the previously-used intelligence agency, only better!"

'Wait, what? So my dad worked for them? So, he's like, a spy?"

Nicolas sighed. "Well, yes, kind of. It's complicated." He paused. "Anyway, back to the city-states…which you don't know about..." He trailed off. "So…Parker will gladly explain it to you!" Nico said quickly, not leaving any room for the guard to object.

"Ugh.." Parker murmured. "Well, in 2091, the U.S. government combined every two or three states to make provinces, for the sake of the budget cut of 2079." After seeing a slightly confused look on Xavier's face, Parker replied. "You'll hear about that later. States like Maine and Vermont and New Hampshire were combined, as well as Florida, Georgia, and, well, you get the point. But that's irrelevant."

"Anyway, you were raised to be social, fun, and secretly dangerous. The social and fun of course coming from your mother, the other from your father. You were introduced to training when you were only five, such a young age. Of course I know this only from Nico telling me, so I'll let him tell you the rest." Xavier could tell neither of them wanted to talk, but he couldn't tell if that was out of laziness, fear, or some other factor.

"You're probably wondering about the training part of that. Any chance you want to know about the social and fun part?" Parker laughed without humor, taking a chance. Xavier gave him a look, and the guard nodded gravely.

"Didn't think so. Well, your dad worked for the CPAA, as you already know, but he wasn't in a type of position you would think of. He, um, got the job done, if you know what I mean. The government sent him out on all sorts of jobs, some to kill, some to torture, anything of that kind. But out of all of those missions, he never failed. Until they decided to turn on him, that is. Him and you."

"Getting off topic. He trained you five times a week in the basement of your house. He taught you stuff like how to fight, how to defend yourself and others, but best of all, he taught you how to remain in control. You see, he was a respected man among the U.S. government. Nobody on Earth dared to cross paths with him, and when they found out he had a spy as a son, that made them all the more horrified. The thing is, Xavier, Nico and I have come to a conclusion. The Bureau didn't take you because you somehow found out something. No, they're much too smart for that. They could've just sent out a mission over the course of years to track you down and kill you. They kept you for something bigger, something better. Xavier, they took you as a weapon."

11

Confusion spun throughout Xavier's head. "What do you mean, a weapon? Look, I'm sorry, maybe I used to be useful, but right now I don't know anything, I'm not anything special and I'm certainly not a weapon!" He said towards Parker.

Simon Parker certainly knew he wasn't about to argue with Xavier on this. Being hard headed was one thing, but Xavier seemed to take it to a whole other level when he didn't want to believe something.

"Yes you do, Xavier. Believe Parker, I've been told things that you've done since you awoke. Of course, I know everything from the hallway to the bathroom." Nico said. Xavier was confused. *How did he know, and when did Parker have time to tell him?*

Seeing this, Nico explained himself. "When you blacked out, he gave me a call and explained everything. Aside from the fact that Project X was my own nephew. You sort of left that part out." he said, glaring at Parker.

Xavier still refused to believe it. "No, I'm not special anymore! I don't have any skill, and in case you don't remember, I barely remember anything from my old life aside from that flashback!" he yelled at Simon and Nico, who, at which he was surprised, seemed to not be getting any of this. The pair shared a look before Parker announced he was getting a drink from the kitchen. He went over to the stainless steel fridge and got out a water bottle.

The patient stood up, wanting to let Nico know he really didn't know anything. After all, who would know what he knew better than himself?

Parker came back with three bottles and tossed one to Nico, who was still laid back on the couch. He came up in front of Xavier, and held out a hand with one in it. Another hand was behind his back properly, like a waiter in a fancy restaurant would be when offering wine. Xavier declined the water bottle, pushing the guard's hand away smoothly but gently, silently saying that he didn't want one. In response, Parker pulled out his hand from behind his back and produced a butcher knife much bigger than the length of his hand to elbow. He swung at the patient with it and, in shock, Xavier pulled back. His brain took a few quarters of a second to wrap around the situation, but then he let his movements flow out without thought.

The patient kicked back one of the guards knees, bringing him down. He quickly grabbed Parker's wrist of the hand that held the knife and brought it back behind his head. Xavier grabbed the knife and held it up to Simon's neck. Nico sat still on the couch, watching contently. All that Xavier could think of know was the fact that Parker had turned on him. *I was wrong to trust them, either of them!* He thought it while watching Nicolas with a careful eye.

A surprising laugh came from Parker, one that signaled he was impressed. He reached back and grabbed the knife out of Xavier's rock hard hand. Xavier let him grab it, too shocked by everything to think about it. Not to be wrong, he was still highly on guard. Parker stood up and mimicked brushing the dirt off of his pants.

"See, I told you! You still have it! A little rusty, but we can work on that," Parker said, amused. Suddenly Xavier understood. *This was a test!* He thought. *All of that for nothing*? His rage boiled up to his mouth.

"Parker, you little-! I could've killed you, what would you have done then? Huh? Don't EVER try anything like that again!" he yelled at the both of them. Xavier was extremely mad at this while being very worried. *What if I would've killed Parker?* He thought. Suddenly he was very angry at himself for even doing that. *Out of all the things he could have done, why did he have to hold the knife to his throat? It wasn't my fault*! The patient thought. *But maybe Parker's right. Maybe I did know a little about fighting before I lost my memory. No, I'm still mad at him. Look at what he just did!*

"Of course, of course," Nico replied for Simon, who sat himself down on the couch. "We simply wanted to see if you remembered anything. Call it testing your instinct, if you wish." He said in a cool and smooth voice. Nico seemed to know everything that was going on at the moment with no confusion at all.

"Okay, but this will not happen again!" Xavier confidently announced to them both, confident in his words. If they denied, he would have to make sure it didn't happen. After all, if he could do what they said he could, wouldn't he be able to handle 2 barely trained men?

"So," Nico said, breaking the silence. "What do you desire for dinner, Xavier? I suppose you'll want the usual?" He caught himself right after he said it and sighed. "The usual, which consists of red peppers, olives and such wrapped in a dough outside, and then baked for thirty minutes. You'll like it, you always have." Now, Xavier didn't know what to expect. Nobody had told him what he liked and what he didn't like, and that's something he strangely didn't remember.

"Why don't I remember anything?" he blurted out.

Nico and Parker, who were walking to the kitchen, turned back and looked at him, and then each other. Nico shrugged, signaling that it was Parker's turn to answer. The guard sighed and walked over to Xavier.

"That's one of the things we discussed while you were out. We've come to the conclusion that they wiped it completely out. As for recovering it, I don't know how that's going to go. But, the good news is that you seem to be remembering things, like in your blackout. It's slow, but a good start nonetheless. Now, I don't know about you, but I'm absolutely starving! Lets go eat!" Parker said with joy as he rushed over to the kitchen island. There Nico had gotten out a myriad of ingredients to make dinner. Xavier walked over, obviously stunned by the recent events. From breaking out of a secret operation to discovering they wiped his memory, all in one day's work.

"You know," Nico shouted at Xavier from the kitchen. "Most people couldn't handle the stress of what you've gone through today." Xavier stepped towards the island and leaned his hands on it. He smiled sarcastically.

"Now, do you always know what I'm thinking?" The patient asked with a hint of sarcasm in his voice. Nico replied with a smile and spun around to grab a kitchen knife out of the knife holder. Seeing this, Xavier tensed up and prepared for a fight.

"Chill out, I'm just using it to cut the food. See?" Nicolas questioned as he cut the peppers into strips. The patient calmed down, but he was still on guard.

———

"Mm, this is so good!" Xavier said while shoving a mouthful of food into his mouth. He hadn't realized how hungry or thirsty he was until he got the chance to eat. It felt as though he hadn't eaten in forever, and it was the very first meal of his life.

Nico had brilliantly prepared a food that tasted like heaven to the patient. He called the course "Stuffed Mini Peppers," which seemed too plain for a food that good, Xavier had decided. It'd taken less than an hour to prepare, and it was well worth the wait. Peppers, salt, olives, and anchovies burst to life in his mouth. The only problem was that he was beginning to get tired. Very tired.

"Hey, Nicolas," he said after finishing the last pepper. "Where am I sleeping tonight?" He asked while taking a sip of his wine. Nico looked up, seeming to be in deep thought.

"Parker, would you mind sleeping in the guest bedroom while Xavier takes your room for the night? I'd like him to get a chance to get familiar with the house he's already seen before seeing any more." To this Parker nodded sleepily while announcing he was headed off to bed, and bade everyone a good night.

"Xavier, let me show you where you're going to be sleeping," Nico said, dabbing his lips with a napkin. He stood up and went over to the room in which Parker had gone earlier. Xavier's uncle opened the door and let Xavier walk in.

12

Xavier entered the room and looked around. It was a medium sized room, though about the size of Org's bathroom times two. A small, low bed was sitting in one corner, underneath a window giving away a view of the moonlight hitting the desert. It was something he could only imagine being in a Van Gogh painting, he thought. Or, was it? *How would I know?,* he questioned himself. But by then he didn't really care; all he cared about was sleep.

"Well, you'll stay here for tonight," Nico said re-announcing his presence. Xavier looked over and nodded. A thought came to him.

"I don't really have any, um, clothes or anything to wear tomorrow," he stated awkwardly.

Nico considered this before telling Xavier he could borrow some of Parker's clothes for the upcoming day.

"Well, goodnight, and welcome back," Nico said before closing the door behind him. The patient went over to the bed and sat down. He then adjusted the pillow and crashed into a comfortable sleeping position, pulling the thick blanket over him. It was surprisingly cold in the room, a difference from the warm kitchen, living room, and outside. The air vents came to mind, sending shudders through him.

He replayed all of the day's events through his mind. He knew that waking up in that dark room would be one of his recurring nightmares for a very long time. The small, humid vents that barely held him were certainly enough to make any sure man claustrophobic. Finding Parker had been a miracle, he decided. Without him, Xavier would've never gotten out of that horrid place.

Xavier's thoughts could have gone on forever, and

they seemed to, until sleep overtook him.

13

"Okay, get up!" a voice dictated to him as he lay on the hard, concrete ground.

Xavier opened his eyes and surveyed his surroundings. Above him, a man, one older than himself, towered and stared down at him, hands on hips. If Xavier didn't know any better, he would say that the man looked agitated.

The pair was in a basement, but not a normal one. This room, which was more of a tunnel now that he could see, was all made of steel with no windows in it. The only exit that seemed to exist were two heavy-looking, closed doors.

"Didn't you hear me, come on, Xav, we've got to continue," the voice rang out again. The man above him now had compassion on his face, but on his body he wore a loose, gray t-shirt and tan, khaki shorts.

"Uhh…," was all Xavier could manage as his eyes struggled to adjust to the bright lighting. The man extended his hand, and before he knew it, Xavier had grasped it and pulled himself up.

A big flash of light struck him in the face before he was suddenly several feet away, watching the pair. *A man and a boy, man and child. Stranger and-wait, is that me?* The other Xavier looked younger, yet still just as strong. *Maybe he is around fifteen, but no more,* Xavier thought. As his mind was still struggling to understand his new surroundings, a thought triggered in the recesses of his memory.

This must be another vision, he thought. *One of those like the one in the desert. Of course it is, what else would it be?* He silently argued with himself. Meanwhile, the fifteen year old and the man resumed their activities.

"Now, let's try this exercise, shall we?" the man questioned while handing the fifteen year old a semi automatic handgun, one which looked too dangerous for a kid of that age to be handling. Then again, Nico did tell him about the training his dad had given him. *Wait, was it Nico or Parker telling me about it?* Xavier questioned. He finally reached the conclusion that the man was in fact, his dad. Then, the room's noise died.

Joseph Hider pointed with his right hand towards the end of the tunnel, to eight dummies with targets on them. He gestured to them, and both of the Xavier's understood. The young fifteen year old grabbed the gun, instantly knowing what to do. He turned around calmly and faced the ground opposite that of the dummies.

Joseph pulled a pair of ear buds out of his pant pocket and plugged them into his ears.

"Shoot!" he yelled while watching the targets carefully. A fifteen year old Xavier turned around like a bullet and took a fraction of a second to aim before firing. Eight bullets pierced the air, followed by obnoxiously loud gun shots that echoed throughout the tunnel. The sound rang through the air to the patient's ears, which it easily pierced. Once again, sound dragged Xavier down to his feet, tugging at his head, covering his ears. Unbearable pain vibrated through his ears, making his hearing temporarily shut down. It was like the echo continued until it had finally succeeded in making Xavier sure of the most excruciating pain he had ever felt or remembered.

After the ring in his ear had settled to a tolerance he could deal with, Xavier looked up, wondering why the fifteen year old wasn't writhing on the floor like he had been. A closer look at his ears revealed tiny ear buds that seemed to help with deflecting the sound away from his ears.

The man and his son took off walking down the tunnel as a pair as they took out their ear protectors. The ghost, as Xavier had decided to call himself in these visions, followed. He had to hurry up off of the ground and jog up to catch the pair, who were rapidly walking towards the targets. They neared the targets and walked to the first one.

The first target had been pierced right in the middle, a direct hit. Joseph nodded at his son approvingly. They moved on to the second one. This target had been shot right to the left of the center, but it would still be a kill shot. One after another they examined, and all of the bullet marks were either in the dead center, as perfect as they could be, or right outside of it. Either way, his father was satisfied.

"Good, son, I think we're done for the day," Joseph said while walking towards the door with his son at his side. The younger Xavier looked professional and alert, like he had been trained to be. The patient, on the other hand, couldn't believe that the young, highly trained child was himself in a former year.

Joseph Hider reached the door and reached into his left pocket, fumbling for his keys. However, instead of keys, a switchblade knife was produced from his hand. He turned to his right, where young Xavier was already in motion. The fifteen year old kicked his father's knees from under him, making the older patient remember what he'd done to Parker just hours ago. Joseph was on his knees at the ground in a matter of seconds. Xavier had pulled his gun that he still had and pointed it towards his father.

"Nope, that was all wrong," Joseph instructed, standing up. Xavier lowered his gun and sighed.

"How was that wrong? I did it just like you taught me to! What's wrong with that?" fifteen-year-old Xavier yelled angrily. The young boy was agitated now, seeming to never do anything right on this exercise.

His father sighed. "Son, you know exactly what you did wrong." After seeing his son shake his head back and forth, he continued. "What would happen if I brought the knife to your face as you kicked my knees? You'd be dead. Boom! Just like that. You've got to rest your weight on your back left foot and jab with your right foot at their knees. Meanwhile, you still have to be on guard for everything, including any weapons they might have on or near them. Understood?" Young Xavier nodded; he secretly rolled his eyes, but made certain that his father didn't see it.

Joseph located a key from within his pocket and unlocked the doors. Xavier walked out, followed by Joseph. By the time the patient could follow, everything was blacked out.

Xavier jerked awake. Dawn was barely peaking over the edge of the windowsill as he looked out of it. A dull, metallic ping of metal hitting the floor rang out to him as he looked towards the door. The air vent above him rushed cold air into his room, which sent shivers down his spine. Realizing he must've thrown his shirt off during the night, his eyes frantically scoured the room for it.

He eased put of bed and ambled across the room only to realize that his shirt was doused in recent sweat, making it un-wearable. Xavier cursed under his breath as he opened the door to the big room, not caring what he looked like.

The sound of the waterfall lightly flowing greeted him as he drowsily walked into the room. The other two inhabitants of the building were in the kitchen, seeming to be arguing over what to make. Parker reached down to grab the pan, put it on the flat top stove, and proceeded to plant his hands on his hips while staring at Nico. In return, Nico didn't budge. He kept arguing that eggs would be a helpful object for Xavier's body, while Parker debated that flavor was everything.

Xavier walked up within feet of the pair, still unnoticed. He let out a cough, letting them acknowledge his presence. Nico and Parker's heads jerked over, and the argument stopped.

"My, you're awake early," Parker said before receiving a scowl from Nico.

"Of course, you idiot. He's always awake early," he muttered, trailing off quietly.

Parker swung his head over to look at Nico. "Excuse me, what was that? I'm sorry for being the person who actually helped rescue Xavier from that place! Remind me, where were you when he needed us?" He was clearly annoyed now, but he knew he had gotten the upper hand on Nico. Xavier watched, stunned. He raised his eyebrows at the tow, wondering what could have possibly set the two off.

14

"Guys, cut it out!" After he had enough of Parker and Nicolas going on and on about him, Xavier finally had to separate the two, who were as close to blows as he had ever seen them. They had gone on about helping Xavier, Parker finally getting the better end by reminding Nico that he'd not been there to help Xavier. This resulted in Nico angrily storming into his own room a few seconds after.

After a few minutes of rummaging through piles of documents and folders, Nicolas finally found what he was looking for. He smiled as his picked it up. Then he darted back into the kitchen, anxious to show the others what he had found.

"Look," he said as he slammed the pile of photos onto the island in the kitchen. Xavier and Parker looked down at the scattered pictures. Many of them were of Xavier, when he looked much younger. Most of them, he realized, had Nicolas and Joseph pictured as well.

"Nico, what are these?" Xavier asked in awe as he looked through the pictures. He picked up one and held it in his hand.

This photo was different. Xavier was in the middle of two men. On his left was Joseph and his right was Nico and another man he didn't recognize. They weren't in a row, like a normal family would pose in a picture. Xavier had his back to the camera, and at closer look he was about ready to shoot a bow at a target a great distance down a field. The other men were watching him, seemingly unaware of the photo being taken. They all had looks of concentration on their faces, as Nico did now. Xavier knew he should remember something of this moment; he tried desperately to bring this out of the storage part of his brain. It was a long shot, he knew that. If he could retrieve anything about a particular moment, or about anything, on command, what would stop him from remembering everything else?

"I remember this one vividly," Nico voiced, breaking Xavier out of his trance. "Derrin and I," he pointed towards the unknown man in the picture, "had just gotten you and your dad out of a Chinese prison. Well, no. It wasn't a prison as much as it was a few nutcases keeping you hostage. Oh, believe me, I never heard the end of it. You and your father apparently had things," he used air quotes, "'under control.' Yeah, it sure seemed that way when we arrived. They had you chained. Yes, chained to the very chairs you were sitting in. We got there, only to find you and your dad brutally beaten, but still living nonetheless. Needless to say, after that incident, Joseph pounded your training like never before. If the Chinese didn't kill you, the training should have. Thankfully, it didn't. But, and it's just my opinion. I think he was scared."

Xavier looked up quizzically. "Of what?"

Nico was still examining the photo, but kept sneaking glances up at Parker, almost to say, ha, I won. In return, Parker just gave him a snide look. Nico looked down at the picture while grinning at his victory. Xavier just rolled his eyes at this.

"I think he was scared of losing you. I mean, you were his pride and joy. He wouldn't mind bragging to the local police about you and how you could probably kick their butts in a fight any day. Of course, this didn't exactly help him make friends, but, you know, the CPAA helped out with that."

"Yeah..." Xavier trailed off in thought.

Half of an hour later, breakfast was made. Nico set out plates on the island while Xavier and Parker cooked the food. The plates were not the hard part, ironically. Of course, setting the silverware like Nico did would require hours from an untrained waiter, but this was an exception. Nico, Xavier was intrigued to find out, was the owner of the largest and supposedly 'best' restaurant chain in the world, Athena's Garden. It wasn't fast food; rather, it was a highly classical restaurant focused on keeping the ideal tradition of Greek food, architecture, and atmosphere. Almost every major city in the world had one, and almost everybody in the upper class had made it their permanent dining location.

In the kitchen, the others had worked together to make a dish consisting of freshly cut oranges, peaches, and pastries fit for a king. Kourithes, a Greek pastry, obviously inspired by Nico, had rounded out the meal. Kours, as Nico claimed to call them, were glorified shortbread cookies that melted in Xavier's mouth.

Mmm," he sighed again as he tasted his first bite. He picked up his glass of just-squeezed orange juice and took a sip. "This is the best food I've ever tasted!" Xavier exlaimed with delight.

Parker agreed quietly by nodding his head. "Yes," he muttered. "It's very good." Parker had been virtually silent since his fight with Nico.

After Parker was excused to use the bathroom, Xavier took his chance to question Nicolas about this. "What's with him now?" he asked.

Nico looked up from his plate towards Xavier. "Don't worry," he brushed it off. "He's always like this after we have an argument. He'll be back to normal in no time. Just leave him alone for a few hours."

Xavier took this in pondering the relationship between Nico and Parker. "He doesn't seem like the type of person to get mad after a fight," Xavier remarked.

Nico nodded. "No, he's not exactly mad. I think he's just, well, thinking. Thinking about what we said to each other, probably regretting every word of it, too." This made Xavier feel bad.

"Well, maybe I should go talk to him," he said as he stood to head in the direction of Parker's room. Quickly Nico was out of his seat and in front of Xavier.

"Oh, no. No. No. No. Don't go talk to him now. He'll explode on you and then it will just make him feel worse later. Trust me on this, Xav." Xavier looked down before nodding. He decided a change of subject was needed.

"Tell me about this Derrin, the one in the photo." The two returned to their breakfast and sat down. Nico nodded and shoved a spoonful of fruit into his mouth.

"Derrin Legg is a family friend of ours. Well, rather, he's a son of a family friend of ours. His dad, William Legg, has helped us through tough times. Derrin grew up with Angelica, they were actually neighbors for the longest of times. He has a sister; we call her Ally. The cutest little thing, you'll like her once you meet her again."

In his head, Xavier pictured a happy family, with a sixteen year old son, four year old daughter, and two happily married parents.

"Does he know about me?" Xavier asked Nico, who had finished eating.

"Yes," he wiped his face with a napkin. "He knows about everything. Well, everything since I came up here, which was about a few days ago. You see, I have a home down by where he lives, in Independence. He lives somewhat close to me. Just a young kid, but he's every bit as talented as you are, my friend. Works for your dad as well. You'll meet him sooner or later."

"Nico," Xavier put his plate by the sink to be washed later, "Where is my dad? Do you even have a lead?" He shook his head at this new found respect and care for his dad's well-being. For all Xavier knew, his father could be dead, but he wouldn't care. Or at least, he didn't think he would. How could he miss somebody he didn't even remember meeting? Or maybe he remembered some things, but nothing that could preserve his memory permanently. This was a problem, because it bothered him immensely.

15

"What do you mean, you LOST him?" CPAA co-director Alex Mansur screamed at her two co-workers. They were inside of her office, the three of them. Derrin "Barton" Legg had been sitting in a chair opposite Alex's desk, while agent Raphael Sandriel paced around the room.

Derrin Legg was a tall, muscularly built agent of the CPAA, almost at the top rank. He almost always dressed in a suit, as was Raphael, making all of the women swoon over him. All except Alex.

Alex "Spark" Mansur, as she was known by all of

her peers in the same building, was notorious for her ability to change from happy to irate in a matter of seconds. Everyone assumed that was where her nickname came from, but those closer to her knew different. As a kid, Alex was in a house fire which had killed both of her parents. The fire, she said, was caused by a spark plug overheating. She was at such a young age when this happened that the only mark she had of that night was a scar on her lower left arm. Alex often hid it, though, for fear that it showed her only weakness to any co-worker.

Raphael shook his head at how unbelievable it sounded. "I don't know. He just disappeared from our radars. This was about a few days ago," he sighed, knowing that this news would only enrage Spark more. Surely, it did.

Spark backhanded a lamp sitting on the edge of the table, and it flew into the wall and then slammed onto the floor. The light bulb shattered, leaving traces of glass on the floor. Derrin only rubbed his hand over his face in an exasperated fashion. He let out a huge breath before speaking.

"He disappeared. When we sent him with to his last mission, he disappeared, plain as that. There's no if's, and's, or but's about it. We lost him. Now we can either work on getting him back, or--," Derrin managed to get out before Spark cut him off.

"No! I'm giving the orders here!" She yelled in frustration. "Of course we are getting him back, you idiots! He's the best agent we have, and that means he's over you two! I want every person we have at this base out to *every place he has been*, and I want them looking for him. Take whatever weapons you have to. I just want him found by tomorrow!" Spark annunciated the last three words each individually for effect.

The two men nodded their heads slowly. "Yes, but do you know how large the world actually is, Alexandra?" Raphael used her full name, causing both heads to whip around towards him. He stopped pacing and stared at Alex.

"And, even if we did the search, who is to say that he is still there? He could be anywhere in the world by now, and I do mean anywhere," his voice was flat and emotionless as he asked the words.

Alex slowly walked from behind her desk to stand directly in front of Raphael. Her face was inches away from his as she finally halted. Normally, she was considerably shorter, but the high heels she wore on her feet made up for the height difference. Raphael's breathing was level, as was Derrin's. The man lounging in the chair just looked at the pair, unsurprised.

"You listen here and you listen well. I don't care how important any of those men are, and unless they are the president of the United States, they will be out in that country searching for him until he is found. You will keep your computer geeks tracking him to see if he turns up. If he does, send your men there. He must be returned without a mark on him. Understood?" Brutal force came through her voice, though not surprising either of the agents.

The man that was seemingly impossible to intimidate lowered his head and nodded. Raphael walked out, leaving Derrin and Spark left alone. Derrin smirked into his hand, which was covering his mouth.

"That was mean," he said, covering a smile. Secretly, he hated Raphael and loved whenever he stood up to Alex. Whenever he did, she would always lash out at him like a snake attacking its prey, never admitting that he was right and she wrong. One time, in a position like this, Raphael had brought up a point that Alex knew was smart and right, yet she didn't admit defeat. In response, Raphael was forcefully dragged to a holding cell for a five day's of captivity.

The holding cell, known as the Cell to everyone at the CPAA, was an all black cell with no windows except for one tiny window in the door. Inside was humid, with one toilet and no sink. One day was enough to force secrets out of healthy-minded victims, but four days was all it took to get things out of the best of captured soldiers. Luckily, Raphael survived by the mercy of the other guards, who regularly brought him beverages, flashlights, and food. This was, of course, without Alex finding out. Once he had served his penance, Raphael worked to make Spark's life as hard as possible by arguing every point of hers that was wrong. And somehow, Raphael was never sent back to the Cell again.

"They don't pay me to be nice," the woman said as she slowly returned to her chair and sat down. With the ease of an expert, Alex popped up her tablet which connected to a glass keyboard. She looked over at Derrin. "What are you still doing here? Go on now, go away!"

Before Alex could finish, Officer Legg was out of Alex's office and hurrying away towards his own. He sank down in his rotating chair, relieved to be in the peace of his own office.

Two knocks came from the door not minutes after he sat down. With his mind on the situation at hand, he sighed before extending a welcome.

Raphael entered and invited himself to a seat across from Derrin. He started talking even before Derrin acknowledged his presence.

"What would you do if I could find out where Xavier is?" Derrin's head jerked up from his writing pad. A disbelieving look smothered his face. Raphael nodded at his surprise.

"I have a lead, if you're interested. I don't promise much, but it's a start." Derrin's mind was still processing the words he had just heard. He looked at Raphael, waiting for an answer. He took a sip out of a bottle of water he had in his mini refrigerator, waiting for the next vital piece of information to be voiced.

"Okay, you're not going to like this, but the lead I have is William Legg." If he hadn't already swallowed it, Derrin was pretty sure he would've spit out the water he had in his mouth.

"You mean my father?" he questioned Raphael. From his view, Raphael had to be lying. Derrin hadn't spoken to his dad in ages it seemed. Not since he was eighteen; had it really been four years?

Derrin and William Legg had gotten into an argument over a situation that was unpreventable. Derrin had killed a man on a job, one he had been assigned from the CPAA. When he came home, William almost strangled Derrin in defense of his friend, who had apparently been killed hours before. It had been a gunshot, apparently a head wound that had caused the fatality. The explanation from the police was that his son had killed William's friend. The pair hadn't spoken since.

"Yes," Derrin's attention snapped back.

"This part you won't like either, but we have to visit him," Raphael explained in the most casual of tones.

Derrin's hopes of getting out of this had gone from ninety percent to zero in an instant.

"Oh, and get this part," Raphael said while Derrin braced himself. "We have to keep it from Alex."

16

"What do you mean, we have to keep this information from Alex?" Derrin asked in disbelief. The idea was ludicrous, if not crazy and not to mention impossible. Alex knew everything about anything going on involving the CPAA and almost anything involving any of the workers. Keeping anything away from her, especially their absences, would be suicidal and nearly impossible. It was almost as if it was completely out of the question.

"It'll be hard, but we can do it. Do you still have problems with your dad?" Raphael asked. Derrin rolled his eyes, as if the answer was obvious. Derrin was pretty positive that William still hated his guts, and he didn't want to stop by and find out.

"I have people that will cover for us. But if we do this, we cannot communicate with home base and especially not Alex. Is this clear?" Derrin thought about this predicament and then nodded in agreement, knowing there would be dire consequences if this didn't work out.

"Let's go."

———

"Of course I have a plan. Why wouldn't I have a plan?" Nico asked while he finished loading the silver dishwasher. Xavier stared at him.

Nico put the last plate in and sighed in defeat. "Okay, maybe I don't have a plan. So what? I do have a lead, though. I've been working on this case; your dad's, I mean." Once again he surged to his room and returned this time with a folder. The manila folder over-flowed with papers. This drew Xavier' s attention immediately.

"So, William Legg has been working on your father's absence since you've both been gone. He thinks he's gotten a lead, but that man has gotten crazier than a box of hammers since his son left him." Xavier gave him a cross look. "Okay, okay. We can call him if you'd like. See what he's found. Does that sound okay?"

"No!" Xavier hurriedly blurted out. "This is my father we're talking about. Look, I know I don't remember much of him, but, but,--" he stammered while searching for the right words. Having no memory, not even an inkling of a past was beginning to wear Xavier's patience down. He had no leads himself, so he was completely reliant on these two men who he felt had his best interest at heart. Only time would tell.

"But you still want to save him. Yes, please spare me the sap story." Nicolas rapidly flipped through the pages in the folder. "Ah ha!" he muttered as he pulled out a paper and lowered it onto the immaculate granite countertop.

"This," he slammed his hand onto the paper; "is a fax from Will. It's just about all that he's found. Which, as you can see, is not much. But, umm," he ran his finger down the length of the paper until he found what he was looking for. "Here, read this." Xavier looked down at the print on the paper.

"Nicolas, my trusted friend, I've found that Joseph's disappearance was not initiated from the United States government. Rather, I've provided you with everything that has led me to believe Joseph and Xavier were both taken by the same person, or, rather, the same agency. I do not believe it is the work of one man, but perhaps one central controller. But if you do find this place, be warned. We have no idea of what is housed in there, but we do know that it is highly dangerous. Do NOT attempt to go there alone."

Xavier looked up, one phrase making him think. "PARKER!!" he screamed loudly enough to catch Simon's attention, who was still in his room off the far end of the kitchen. He hurriedly whispered to Nico, careful not to lose his train of thought.

"Nico, do you think that wherever I came from, that's the place that took my dad and I? If so, Nico, that's only a few miles away from here! We can get him out! Nicolas, this is our chance!" Joy overflowed in his voice.

"No," Nicolas said with certainty, "that place, I don't know why you were there, but it's just a holding place. Or at least as far as the locals say. Somewhat of a hospital for lost causes, as I've understood. I don't know who is permitted there, but trust me. It's not as bad as to take the two top agents of the United States government! Maybe somebody anonymously dropped you off there, but it's no threat!"

Xavier spoke quietly and harshly. "But Nico, what if you're wrong? He could be there!" Nico only rolled his eyes.

As if on cue, Parker came out, looking tired and uncaring. "Making plans without me?" he directed harshly at Nico. If there was one thing Xavier couldn't have, it was the only two people he knew fighting like this.

"Parker, stop. We have a lead, one that can help my dad. You are either in, no fighting with Nicolas, or you're out. Pick one. Now." Simon Parker, for once, was speechless. He wasn't used to so much control from Xavier, but then neither was Nico. It shocked both of them.

"Ok, I'm in." Xavier shook his head. "Good. Now read this." He slid the paper over to Parker, who grabbed it smoothly. He shook his head after reading it.

"This is some hardcore stuff. Are you sure you can handle it? No disrespect, but you don't exactly remember a much that can help us."

Nico covered for him. "He remembers enough, and that's all that matters."

Xavier was deep in thought while they were talking. Confusion raced through his mind, taking over. Unanswered questions loomed, threatening to drive him mad.

"Nico, I thought you said you knew all about the Bureau? Didn't you say it was driven by some lunatics? Will somebody please fill me in on what apparently I missed because I was being fed lies?" Now anger flew through him like a rocket in the sky. He didn't like being lied to, he had at least figured that much out.

Nico nodded to Parker, giving him a silent signal. "Xavier, I'm sorry, but we couldn't have put so much stress on you the first day, and--,"

"Wasn't that MY choice?" Xavier yelled while turning around to pace the room. He sighed and came back, trying to cool down the harsh tone in his voice. "I need answers and quick. Will somebody just please tell me what the hell is going on here?" he said with rage. Parker and Nico stared at him in shock. From the time they had found him yesterday to now, they had yet to hear him get angry to such a degree as this. His mother had taught him that proper language was everything when talking to anybody, but he seemed to not remember it. Either that or he didn't care, but it was still disconcerting to Xavier's companions.

Snapping out of his shock, Parker spoke first. “I'm sorry, Xav. The truth is, I met Monroe, he convinced me to join him, and I don't really know anything about the place. They just told me to do a job, and I did it. I guess I was just broken down after you left. But whoever they are, they're not the United State government. And you're here now, which is all that matters. Right?” His voice was smooth and convincing. Xavier nodded while not really paying attention to anything being said after his questions were answered. His mind was preoccupied but, however, put the puzzle pieces together.

“We have to go see William,” he concluded aloud. Nico and Parker shared a glance, and Simon began to protest.

“Xavier, you know we can't-,” but he was cut off abruptly by Nico. He looked Xavier dead in the eyes while he replied.

“Okay. We'll go.”

17

“What do you mean, 'we'll go'? We're definitely not

going anywhere!" Parker exclaimed with force. Although he sounded very convincing, he knew himself that he could convince nobody in that room when they wanted to do something. Nico looked at Parker with a discriminating glance, one that would make even the most emotionless person crack. Parker had seen this look before, but it still scared him. He sighed, nodded and gave up, although unwillingly.

"So," Xavier said, breaking the silence. "How do we get to there from here? Do we, like, drive to an airport or something?" he asked quizzically.

The other two turned to look at him. Nico was the first to respond. "Of course not. I have a jet that can fly us there. Get with the times."

Well then, Xavier thought at the harsh words. He didn't know if Nico was being overly sarcastic or brutally honest. Maybe he did need to "get with the times." Then again, hadn't he only been gone for about two months? Was two months enough to miss *that* much? How much could happen in to this world in such a short time?

Within an hour that consisted of a phone call and agonizing waiting, the residents of the small, desert village saw a heavy bullet-looking plane cover the sky towards them. The sound was loud enough to draw some villagers out of their huts when it landed on a stretch of smooth desert land behind Nico's house.

Xavier ran over to the doors and threw them open, hoping to catch a glimpse of the maker of the monstrous sound. He dashed out, sprinting into the open expanse of land. When he didn't see anything, he ran around the large house and looked around. In the air was a gigantic bird, a metal one at that. It produced a large sound, if a sound can be called large. It was extremely loud; it spread across the whole village, and Xavier was sure the people at the Org. would be able to hear it. He knew himself that that was an exaggeration, but it helped to exaggerate when his father was missing and his best friend and uncle spent most of their time fighting each other.

It landed with ease, pulling to a stop a quarter of a mile behind Nico's house.

Xavier was smitten: he had never seen an airplane like this before, at least not one that he remembered. It wasn't just an airplane, though. It certainly wasn't one like he remembered.

The bird was pitch black, but with no wings. Rather, it was like a bullet piercing the air, only with a giant turbine protruding from the back. When it came close to scraping the ground, two metallic prongs attached to wheels grazed the ground with ease. They sort of reminded Xavier of the feet of a bird, reaching down to grab a fish out of a lake. Or an owl, swooping down onto the forest floor to stealthily catch an unsuspecting mouse.

Nicolas came outside and tried shouting over the roar of the plane. After failing at that, he ran up to Xavier and shouted in his ear.

"You need to come in and get ready to leave!" Though, all Xavier could get out was "you", "come", and "leave." So when Nico jogged off towards the house, the patient took that as his cue to follow and did. They went in to find Parker, followed by two black suitcases. Xavier eyed them curiously.

"This is just my stuff. I'm preparing for however long we have to stay there before we return," he explained. Nico came in from shutting the back door, which Xavier didn't know had existed until Nico had just used it.

"What about me?" he asked as he passed by them to get to his room, which was right by the guest bedroom Xavier hadn't seen before. He came to the conclusion that he had been too tired when he headed off to bed to even notice it.

Xavier heard a distant cry. "Xavier, come help me pack!" It sounded to Xavier as if it came from Nico's room. He sighed and complied, having no idea of the disaster that lurked just behind the door.

Much to his surprise, Nico's room was not a trashcan of litter, such as paper plates, dirty clothes, and pizza boxes like he expected. Nico said that he hired one of the town locals to clean for him. Xavier thought about this and decided that it wasn't such a bad idea. It was actually a novel idea, quite clever indeed. Xavier just wasn't quite sure how smart Nico was yet.

After what had most definitely been the longest hours of Xavier's new memory, everyone was packed. All except Xavier, who had no clothes except for the pants he wore and the shirt he had borrowed from Parker. It was a bit small on him, but it was better than no shirt. A man came from the plane outside to take their bags, and Nico handed them to the man with surprising normalcy. *This must be a usual thing for him,* Xavier decided.

Pull-down stairs came from the plane, and Xavier, Nico, and Parker strode up them. Xavier looked ahead anxiously.

Inside, it was like a lounge meets Hollywood party. Colored lights hung decoratively from the ceiling, and red leather couches straddled the bottom of the outside walls. A table with a display of every drink ever known to man was plopped down in the middle, so out of place it looked like it belonged there. A wall separating the pilot's and the rider's area's stood guard, with a curtain marking an entry way between the two areas. Xavier was in awe as he entered the lounge. Nico was second behind him, and he had to nudge him forward to remind him to keep walking.

They sat down, and Nico handed out gum to the two other passengers. Xavier accepted the gum with a puzzled look on his face.

"Chew it while we take off and land. It helps. Trust me," Parker said while taking the crinkling wrapper off of his gum. A few minutes passed, and as the scent of cinnamon filled the cabin air, Xavier was wishing he had taken Parker's taking off advice. Other than that, it was a peaceful two-hour flight to Independence.

On the other hand, Derrin and Raphael's flight was not as pleasant.

"Please fasten your seat belts as we are experiencing mild turbulence," a cheerfully worried voice rang out over the intercom. Derrin hung onto the edges of his seat as hard as he could, while praying to not die. Raphael looked up, woken from his slumber.

"Please don't let me die, please don't let me die, please don't let me die...," Derrin kept repeating over and over again, much to Raphael's annoyance. Raphael rolled his eyes and quietly fastened his seat belt as he was told. He reached under his seat to grab a can of nuts that he had packed for the flight to Independence. The CPAA agent popped the lid open and reached in to grab a peanut. The plane suddenly jerked to the left, causing him to spill the contents of the container all over the floor. A string of curses were sent out of his mouth as he closed the empty container and put it under his seat again, not bothering to pick up the scattered debris. Derrin didn't seem to notice, though; he was too worried about dying. Raphael laughed at him lightly, remembering how he used to feel on planes. This flight, however, had him convinced that Derrin would never get over flying, especially with turbulence.

"I think I'm going to be sick," Derrin scattered the words out of his mouth and into the air like they were poison.

18

"Well, where is it?" Parker asked while worrying. Xavier scanned the perimeters and saw nothing.

"They'll be here," Nico reassured them. Five minutes later, a yellow taxi appeared with "We don't Tax-i you more than we should!" plastered onto the side, pulled up on the curb in front of them. Nico had gotten the attention of the cab driver, so Parker had to congratulate him for getting them all a ride. Xavier scowled at the logo, claiming that it was too cheesy to be seen in. Though, Parker reluctantly followed Nico into the car, and Xavier followed suit, however unwillingly.. Inside was small and compact with the three men shoved in the back with Xavier as a buffer, seated in the middle.

Nico had told the pilot of his plane to land it at the airport nearest to Independence, and that was just two miles from William's house. Independence Airport was a small one, having only two dirt runways. Yet, it was highly convenient for Nico when he flew to see William or when he had used to visit Joseph. One of his best friends oversaw the flights to and from the airport, so in one quick call Nico could have a landing place at the ready.

The ride to William's house was short but stuffy, with four men in the taxi, three of them squeezed in the back of it. Almost no words were exchanged, other than the short discussion of the payment cost of ten dollars and fifty cents. As soon as the three reached William's house on Rowge Boulevard, Xavier had the strangest sense of dèja vu. The house was somehow vaguely similar to a vision he had imagined in his head. The house appeared to be four stories high and was situated on the side of a large hill. The outside was painted white, while the roof was a light gray. It was a beautiful house, one that looked as old as time but just as well kept.

The floors had windows that gave way to a sneak peek inside of the house, which provided an awe factor. "Thank you," the driver said as the three got out and handed him his money. Nico nodded in reply and picked up his suitcase.

"Well, boys," he said while sighing; "what are we waiting for? Let's go see if anybody is home!" The two followed him up the walk to the house, which shadowed them ominously. It didn't scare Xavier; rather, it gave him the feeling of comfort to know that he had at least seen this place before.

When they reached the door, Parker was the one that set his things down and knocked. It was a few seconds before the door opened a crack.

"Hello?" the man's voice asked quietly as he

peeked out. He saw the characters lined up on his door step and his voice lit up. "Nicolas, my friend! Parker!" Then he saw Xavier, and William froze. He turned his back to the guests and yelled in his house while opening the door. "ALLY! Ally, get down here!"

Xavier looked around before being the last one of them to enter William's house. The house inside was as grand as it was out. A marble staircase divided the room, like the one you would see in a movie. Hallways openly directed observers to different parts of the house, and chairs sat in every corner. The floor was tile, much like the floor at Nico's. The house's interior gave off the air of money, while the outside was the scene of serenity and meekness. It confused Xavier, but not as much as he thought the visit would.

A girl that looked to be in her early twenties came walking by on the second floor, by the railing leading to the staircase. She looked at Nico, then Parker, and finally Xavier. She locked eyes with him for what seemed like blissful hours to Xavier, but they both knew it was only for seconds. This extended gaze did not go unnoticed by the others.

"Xavier!" the girl screeched, though not in a shrill, girly way. It was a sign of happiness, of obvious joy. Assuming this must have been Ally answering William's recent call, Xavier watched the girl fly down the stairs and run over to him. He expected her to stop, but she didn't. She kept her pace and pulled him into a big hug, strangling Xavier. He returned her hug, but it felt natural, like he had done it a million times before. Although, he wasn't too sure that he hadn't.

Ally Legg pulled away, stunned that Xavier was here. The patient gave a shy smile at the girl's excitement. She smiled back, but then her face dropped, as if a bad smell hit her.

"Oh, sorry. I guess you don't remember me," she laughed. "Then this is kind of awkward. I'm Ally, Ally Legg. Your best friend since childhood, if I may add."

———

"Well, what are we going to do?" Derrin angrily screamed at the concierge while Raphael paced. They had just gotten inside of their hotel in Independence, and they had figured out that their room had been overbooked. Although the woman at the front desk had no control over the booked rooms, Derrin needed to have somebody to blame.

The scared worker of the front desk replied timidly, "I'm, I'm sorry, sir, but we must have made some mistake in the booking. I can offer you two weeks plus two days free of charge-"

"NO!" Derrin was beyond mad, he was outraged. The one thing he needed to get done, the one thing he was in charge of, was screwed up because of somebody else's mistake. Raphael would never trust him again, not after this. No matter how hard he begged, this wouldn't get past the older officer, who had stopped pacing and walked up to the desk.

"Perhaps we can arrange a deal with one of the other guests," Raphael asked coolly. The concierge seemed to take better to Raphael's calm and quiet voice over Derrin's loud and obnoxious yelling. She seemed to settle down, riffled from Derrin's yelling.

"I-I mean, I don't know, you would have to ask one of them, I mean, I can't do anything like that, I mean, directly, you know," the young girl stuttered out. Her name tag said Ashley Baron, her last name eerily similar to Derrin's nickname. Derrin had noticed the similarity but was too angered to say anything.

"Ashley," Raphael said in a quiet, soothing voice. "Is there any guest who would consider this?" He stared into her eyes. Ashley thought for a minute.

"Well, maybe Mrs. Calder in room ninety-three, but she is the only one who would even think about trading that comes to mind..." Raphael and Derrin were not around to hear her finish the sentence, as they were already off to room ninety-three, to find Mrs. Calder so they could hopefully have somewhere to sleep for the night.

19

Alexandra Mansur stomped into her assistant's office. Her assistant, by the name of Monica, looked up, startled at Alex's anger. Alex usually waited until she got into her office before she let her anger show.

The CPAA co-director went up to Monica's desk and slammed her hands onto the desk.

"Tell me, Monica," she said with rage, pronouncing each syllable precisely. "Where exactly are agents Derrin Legg and Raphael Sandriel at this current moment?" Monica was on the phone, and she motioned Alex away.

Once she was off the call, Alex came back. "Where did they go?" she demanded of Monica. Her fists slammed onto the desk, a sure sign of anger and pure rage. The assistant looked up, surprised by the unusual question. Then she turned immediately back to work.

"I'm not sure, miss, but I will check now if you'll allow it." Alex quickly nodded, telling the assistant to hurry. After a few tapped keys on a glass keyboard, Monica found something. "Their records show them buying two plane tickets..." Monica muttered while determinedly typing. A few more clicks of manicured fingernails hitting the glass occurred and then a confused look crossed her face. She grabbed her computer mouse and clicked on a link on the screen, one that required a pass code. Monica smiled.

Normally, Monica was on top of every password and key code there was or had ever been in the CPAA building of New York. She had them memorized down to the last semicolon. Whatever anybody thought about changing a code, they came to her with their idea. If they didn't, being fired wasn't the worst thing that could happen to them. Monica, everybody said, was the strictest of all the lower level workers. Of course, she thought of it only as "enforcing the rules".

As it went, this was why Monica was in shock when a red box popped up on her computer screen. "Access Denied." The pair of women stared at the screen, stunned. Monica tried this time a different password, only to no avail. The haunting red box popped up on the screen once more.

Alex's assistant had been trying to open the two agents' profiles, knowing that it would reveal their location. Not only would it reveal their location, it would give way to the secret of why they went without orders.

The main quarters of the CPAA looked after a dozen "agents" as they were called. These were the people designated to do the CPAA's dirty work. In this case, the phrase "dirty work" meant taking care of the major threats to the U.S., the ones not even America's most elite forces could handle. Once done with their usual yearly assignment, agents were brought back to home base in New York. They were treated like saints for the rest of the time until another assignment arose.

Some of them had family, but once they became agents, friends and family were told of the supposed tragic death of their loved one. This was the case, except for the director and his son.

In 2063, the CPAA fell apart. It crumbled to pieces on the ground, specks of dust left for other countries to stomp on. The old director had died, supposedly a brutal car crash. But the whole agency knew better than that. They knew that it was no car crash. He had been murdered, it was that simple. Whoever had carried through with the deed had had a plan, and they had stuck to it. The end result was just as their enemy had hoped. Nobody had a plan, no backup, as everybody should have. Of course, this was kept out of the public eye. Nobody wanted that kind of publicity. It would only send all of the citizens into a worried frenzy.

Then Joseph Hider showed up, willing to take command of everything. None of the agents questioned his lead; nobody had the guts to. Joseph was a demanding figure, it was either his way or no way. Within a year the CPAA was back and stronger than ever. But Joseph wanted more, more than just commanding everybody and seeing over everything. He wanted to help all he could, and he intended to do that. So when he announced that he himself was becoming the lead agent, Joseph heard no objections. Except for that of his son.

Xavier insisted that he would work alongside his dad, which surprised Joseph. But with no objection, he allowed it.

Xavier's first assignment had been to capture a terrorist, one of an elite group the USA had been trying to get for years. Xavier found him without even trying. Not only did he capture him, but he got every answer he wanted out of the captive by using an old method his father had taught him. After the terrorist was of no use,

Xavier shot him in the back of the skull, an instant kill shot. Even his father was impressed at the lack of mercy Xavier had demonstrated. That was his first task, and he had undoubtedly passed.

Within time, Xavier and his father became the number one protectors of the United States government. Not only was it their job to take down threats to their country, it was their duty to protect its leaders as well. Whenever a president went anywhere, Xavier or Joseph were on the scene. Of course, nobody knew it except the people involved. Their covers were just that good.

Bringing herself back to reality, Monica once again tried numerous different passwords, only to ultimately fail. Alex watched in anticipation, only to grow more frustrated with every wrong code. Eventually she stomped back into her office, defeated. Alex sighed and slumped in her chair. She was not ready to admit defeat, but she knew that only one option stood open. In her heart, she knew that this was the only way to find two of her best agents. Her one option was to phone Raphael.

As much as she hated him now, she had once loved the solemn agent. It was before her time of directing the Critical Protection Agency of America, before the time of her hatred of anything half-way done, before she grew tired of everyday life.

They had grown up together, Alex and Raphael. While Raphael was the valedictorian of their high school, Alex, on the other hand, was the rough girl in school, the one that got good grades, yet everybody knew enough to stay away from. They made an interesting pair, everybody admitted. Just nobody said it to their faces. There was only one problem: both had one major secret.

Alex was secretly training for the government as a part of a training program to find suitable agents for hire. On the other hand, Raphael already was one. On the second year of training, when their platoons met each other, it was a sight to be seen. They locked eyes, and in a way, they instantly knew. It was only luck when Raphael got promoted to head agent before Joseph's time of manage, while Alex got moved up to Co-Director of the rapidly falling CPAA. This eventually crushed and shattered their relationship.

Spark Mansur would certainly never admit this, but secretly, she had always loved Raphael; even through the pain of working together. Raphael, on the other hand, had sworn off relationships for the pride of his work. He had already been told that his family thought him dead, which was as bad as piercing a bullet through his head. Raphael had been devastated, heartbroken, even. He wouldn't talk to anybody for days, but eventually he knew he had to work past it.

Furthermore, he had never been the same since.

20

Ally gave Parker and Xavier some time to talk and waltzed into the kitchen. Once she exited through the menacing gateway that led to the kitchen, Xavier stole a glance at Parker. The youngest guard checked his watch and looked around until his eyes met Xavier's. He gave him an odd glance.

"What...?" he trailed off, knowing Xavier was up to something. The ex-patient only smiled as he replied.

"Did you see that? Am I hallucinating?" He laughed as he said it. *There is absolutely no way a girl like that,* Xavier thought, *would be best friends with me.* The sweat doused, poorly dressed Xavier. As he looked down, he did only then just notice that he hadn't taken a shower in he didn't know how long. Sand covered parts of his face from the ride to Nico's, and the blue pants he wore of Parker's were a tad small and didn't match his dark and faded green shirt.

Parker sighed and laughed. He went over to sit on a step on the marble stairs, casually inviting himself while Xavier followed his lead. "Yeah, what's wrong with Ally?" Parker smiled at Xavier while he asked the question. It was apparently no secret between the two about what they both thought of the girl. She was gorgeous, there was no denying it. With her wavy blonde hair and body of a model, the two young men couldn't help but be attracted to her.

Xavier just smiled and shook his head back and forth, tossing away the question. He was in deep thought when Parker answered what the patient was about to ask. "She didn't really think highly of me, though, boy, did she have it in for you. You know, I honestly don't know," Parker sighed and looked down at the floor. Xavier had no trouble sensing something was wrong, and came to the rescue.

"Don't know what?" he asked, hoping to cheer Parker up. Although, Parker's reaction wasn't what he thought it would be. Parker looked up with a devilish grin on his face.

"Don't know what she sees in you!" This got Xavier laughing and he slapped Parker playfully on the shoulder. Simon feigned pain as he was hit. He stood casually and pretended to brush dirt of off his shirt.

"That hurt, you know," he said while joking. Xavier laughed while getting up as well. A weird look came from Parker.

"What?" Xavier asked. Parker once again smiled and replied.

"What are you going to do all day, follow my every move?" Xavier was confused until he thought about that. He followed Parker from the airport to the car, from the car to the house, from the house and sitting down on the stairs, and now his actions even mimicked him while he stood. Xavier admitted that Parker had a point.

"Of course I do," he replied. "I always have a point."

The two men's heads turned to the entryway to the kitchen when Nico called them in. "That's our cue," Parker said as he walked towards the kitchen casually. Xavier groaned and followed. Just another thing for Parker to bug him about later on.

The kitchen was filled with Nico, William, Ally, and Parker all surrounding a table before Xavier walked in. All attention turned towards him as he entered, and Ally was the first to speak up. She walked up to him while talking.

"Xavier, why don't I show you around the house? I'll let you take a shower, too," she motioned to the dirt on his face and arms. Xavier thought for a moment, but then nodded in agreement as he followed Ally out of the room. *Wow, I am a follower today,* he thought. *Of course you're going to be a follower, you idiot, you don't have any memory,* he argued back to himself.

He had to speed walk for a moment to match Ally's fast pace. When he finally caught up to her, she was ascending the marble staircase.

"So," he said as she acknowledged his presence with a smile. "Where are we off to first?" Ally stopped halfway up the stairs and turned towards him.

"First, you, mister, are taking a shower." Xavier gave her a weird look but then continued to follow her up the staircase. Eventually they came up to a regular, wooden door on the second floor. Ally stood back and motioned for Xavier to enter, and he did. He walked in and she stood against the left angle of the doorway.

"I'll be back soon with clothes. I'm sure I can find some around this house. I'm assuming you know how to work the shower, correct?"

Xavier turned around. "Well of course. I may not remember much, but I'm not stupid," he said with a smile. Ally returned the smile and left.

The bathroom was golden compared to the one in

the Org. This bathroom was high off of the ground with a big window on the wall opposite of the door, and the toilet was much better maintained than that of the Org. The sink was a dual sink, meaning that it had two sinks instead of one, and a large mirror right above them rounded out that portion of the room. On the other side of the room was the shower, a large one at that. It was right next to the tub, which was, of course, large also. Strangely, it was the shower that caught his eye. He seemed to remember this, from before some time. This time he didn't bother trying to remember where he knew this, because he knew that he probably had no chance at all of succeeding.

After no time at all, he stripped his tight clothes off and stepped through the reflective glass doors. Much to his surprise, he actually didn't know how to work the shower, though he seemed to figure it out soon enough.

At first, cold water cascaded down his face and eventually snaked its way into the drain. *Ah! Hot water, hot water, I NEED HOT WATER!* He anxiously looked around for the hot water switch, and soon he figured out that he had to turn the knob further left to get what he wanted. However, within seconds hot water strolled out of the shower head and onto Xavier. He sighed, gladly washed his hair out, and soon the water became brown with sand and dirt. It filled him with joy, although he knew it was such a simple victory. That and the fact that he won against a shower.

The patient took his sweet time at standing under the hot water, letting the room steam up. He sighed deeply, as if his problems were deep inside of him and he could let them all go with the release of a deep breath. He would've fallen asleep if he wasn't in heaven.

21

Xavier stepped out of the shower relieved and with renewed confidence. He felt like he had washed away all of his troubles and pushed them down the drain. He felt like a new person.

While stepping on the memory foam bathmat, his eyes roamed the room for a towel. He found one just a few feet away draped over a hook on the wall. Xavier tenaciously took it and wrapped it around his waist. What he needed now was a pair of clean clothes to wear. *It's not like I'm going to wear a towel around my waist when in front of Ally and William. That isn't an option at all.*

When he decided that he had no suitable clothes in the bathroom, he made a start towards the door. Perhaps he could call Parker up to the room and borrow some of his clothes, again. Or maybe Ally would come back with some clothes as she promised. He opened the door and looked around. All areas of the house that were in his line of sight were empty, so he figured that they all still must be in the kitchen or somewhere else downstairs. Xavier stepped out of the bathroom and his foot collided with something soft, and he just about slipped. Luckily, the door frame was steady and there to catch his fall.

He looked down; Ally had kept her promise. On the floor was a fresh set of clothes just waiting for him. Xavier picked them up and hurried back inside the bathroom. He gladly put on the soft silk shirt and shorts and was out the door in minutes. Xavier was almost at the top of the stairs when he stopped and backtracked to the bathroom. When he entered it, he stole a glance in the mirror. His hair was still damp, but it was a mess. It wasn't presentable, at least not to be in front of Ally, or so he thought.

He neatly straightened his hair upwards in a presentable fashion. It didn't look right…too practiced and forma is what he decided it looked like. Then he tried fluffing it, it brought an I'm-not-trying-too-hard feel to his presence. Now he was ready.

Xavier pranced down the stairs and into the kitchen. Six figures were standing around the kitchen table looking at the same kind of maps as before he took a shower. He would've walked up, but six was too many. *There should only be five including me. Why are there seven?* Every head swung over his way to glance at the new person. Xavier saw Ally, William, Nico, and Parker, but there were two strangers-two oddly familiar strangers.

Whenever he got that same feeling about somebody, or anybody, for that matter, he automatically assumed that he had known that person before the Org. It was the only explanation for the amount of people he apparently knew before his memory was wiped clean. These two people were no different. He had the exact same feeling, only this time it was stronger, the strongest it had ever been.

Both of the men were wearing black suits, with ties neatly tucked into them. While one of the men was tall, the other was Parker's height. They looked oddly professional. Like how Xavier imagined himself at his job. Perhaps this was how he knew them; maybe they worked in the same job as he did. Just like his father! He wasn't alone! But he wasn't about to let his guard down so easily. These men could be enemies; it wasn't out of the question. *Why, then, did William let them into his house?* Too many questions flowed through his mind. He wished he could go back to the shower.

"Xavier!" One of the men rushed towards him and embraced him into a hug, bringing back memories of how Parker had taken him in when he first saw him in the bathroom. Xavier feebly returned the hug with suspicion. The other agent pulled back and gave him an odd look. The taller agent approached his colleague and put a hand on his shoulder. The shorter man looked at him, confused.

"Xavier, allow me to introduce ourselves. I am Raphael. This one here is Derrin. We're agents of the Critical Protection Agency of America. We've come to locate and bring you home." The one who was apparently Raphael said. Derrin looked at him, a face of despair crossing over him. His jaw dropped slightly out of sadness, and then he looked like a light bulb clicked. He stepped away from Xavier and went to Raphael.

"We used to be your friends. Your best and most trusted friends, you could say," Raphael said arrogantly. Xavier looked over behind him to Parker, who rolled his eyes at Raphael's remark. Xavier had assumed that Parker had been his best friend. That was what he had been told. Now being told another story didn't really help his confusion much at all. He looked to Nico for confirmation. He just shrugged and sighed.

"You can trust them, Xav. They're friends of William and Ally," William glared at Nico after saying this.

"What was that for?" Xavier asked William. "I saw that look. That means he was either telling a lie or saying something you don't like. Care to explain that?" he asked professionally.

Raphael was looking at William, as was everybody else. Everybody else except for Derrin. Derrin had averted his eyes and, not that Xavier had seen, had never looked at William once in this time period.

Silence pierced the air before Parker spoke up. "Xav, meet Derrin. Derrin Legg. Also, while you're at it, meet William Legg, father of aforementioned Derrin Legg," William and Derrin glared at Parker as he broadcasted this piece of information. "Sorry, but it had to be done." He shrugged and went on to explain more.

"Derrin here, was on an assignment in Europe. His mission was to kill a suspected murderer. You see, this suspected murderer was an agent gone wrong who had been captured by the enemy, his mind toyed with until finally he went mad. And then he was set free. At this point, that was when Derrin stepped in and took action. Of course, William was friends with the ex-agent, so that caused a few family issues. Family issues that I guess you could say resulted in father and son never speaking again. I'm sorry, but that's about all I know about that. Any questions about any of this so far?" Nico asked, as if he expected none. Actually, Xavier did have quite a few questions, but he knew it was no use trying to get anybody to answer them directly.

Derrin was staring at the floor and William was giving a deadly look to Parker. Simon just held his hands up in defense. Xavier could feel the tension in the room; it was like the elephant in the room. Once it was there, nobody wanted to mention it or talk about it. But it was there. Oh, was it there.

22

After minutes of awkward silence, William finally stood up and walked away furiously. Up the stairs he went, presumably to his room or study, Ally had pointed out.

"So, you two, you're siblings?" Xavier was trying to piece together this puzzle. *What a family reunion,* he thought sarcastically.

Derrin nodded. "Yep, in the blood. Sadly," he added an evil grin at his sister, who playfully smacked him in response. It was a relationship that Xavier imagined any brother and sister having, although he knew deep down that that wasn't the case.

Parker walked over to Xavier and leaned his elbow

on the patient's shoulder casually. "So, are you guys going to tell him or should we just keep it a secret for the rest of his life?" Parker asked while still leaning on Xavier. Xavier gave him a weird look, one that said what do you think you're doing? Besides that, he was much more interested in what they weren't telling him. He had his fair share of secrets being kept from him, and he wondered if they were always like that. Simon Parker, the confident and devilishly handsome man who was a master at hiding his feelings and making people think the opposite, Nico, the rich, famous, and sometimes disingenuous millionaire; they both had a certain calm but yet deceitful act to them. He hadn't quite had enough time to gather much about William, Ally, Derrin, or Raphael, although Raphael seemed to think himself above everybody else and tried not to show it. Derrin though, on the other hand, seemed to watch everybody, as if he wasn't a part of the conversation.

Xavier sighed, as he asked the question he felt he had asked a million times that day. "Tell me what?" He looked specifically at Parker to answer.

"So that's a 'tell him' to my question..." Simon muttered. When he didn't go on, Xavier silently nudged him, aching for him to continue.

Raphael sighed, bored, and answered before Parker did. "Xavier, we think we found your father."

Martin Monroe let out a long and exasperated sigh. He had lost his biggest assignment ever, and now his operation was crashing to the ground around him. Along with that, as if it had gotten any worse, the experiment had taken the best guard he had ever had, Simon Parker.

But, despite everything that had gone wrong, he still had one advantage, one that could eventually give him the win. They had Robert Clemons, the 52nd president of the United States of America. Of course, the public would soon realize it in a matter of minutes now, but that was assumingly a precautionary risk. Nobody would be able to track him, what with Xavier and Joseph being missing and all. That was the plan all along. They didn't need him for a weapon, that was merely a bonus that came with the job. Monroe only needed to distract the entire country of the United States, and with that distraction came the abduction of Xavier Hider.

Martin got up and walked confidently out of the room and into a hall. After a few left and right turns and the greetings of a few guards, he arrived in front of a door. He knocked twice; it opened and he walked in.

In the middle of the gray room, a metal chair sat in

the middle with two guards by the sides. In the chair sat their captive, Robert Clemons. He was obviously either knocked out or sleeping, because his head was hanging down to his chest. Monroe walked over to him and slapped him lightly on the cheek to wake him up. Robert's head moved a little and he groaned as he looked up. Relief spread across his face as he saw Monroe. Then he realized he was tied to the chair by the chest.

"Martin! What are you doing here? You've got to help me out here! They're," he nodded his head to the guards "they're watching us," he whispered, as if trying to avoid the guards from hearing. The guards just stared on into space, not moving at all.

"Be quiet," Monroe harshly commanded. Clemons was a strong man, strong, lean, and a leader. He looked odd fashioned in his torn suit, but he did not come across as a man that seemed to get surprised easily. When a look of shock came across his face, Monroe didn't bat an eyelash. Robert opened his mouth to speak, but then thought better of it and closed it.

Martin paced back and forth in front of Robert. "Now, Robert, this is how things are going to work. You are in the Sahel desert, I assume you don't know where that is. For the sake of you, it is right below the Sahara desert. Yes, Africa. A long trip, but worth it for the sake of you. Mind you, the expense was crazy; regardless, what matters is that you're here now. If you don't mind, you can either do everything I tell you and cooperate and go out unscathed, or you can take the hard route. Either way is okay with me, I don't care, personally, what happens to you. Believe me, nobody here does nor ever will. Keep in your thoughts that if you so much as scratch this floor with that chair, my men will beat you into oblivion. It's not even a year old and I would not appreciate it being scratched. Is all of this clear?"

Robert's breathing was fast and repeated now. Monroe could see the fear in his eyes and laughed. "That's a yes then." He looked towards his guards. "Boys, what are you doing? Don't you know that this is the president of the United States? Untie him, let him walk around the room." Both of the guards stared at him, unbelieving. When they didn't move, Monroe said something again. "Now!" He rolled his eyes and got up. Monroe walked out of the room, slamming shut the door behind him. This time he took a left and arrived at two heavy metal doors which required a key code to get through. He typed in "1.0.1.9.5." and the doors slid open with ease.

After surveying the rest of his building, including the Caplar, he went back into his office and sat down heavily in his chair. He didn't need all of this stress, but he certainly couldn't let anybody else know of his worry.

Monroe was deep in his thoughts when his phone rang. He jumped but then answered it.

"Hello?"

"Monroe? This is agent Baron. Ashley Baron."

"Oh, how good it is to hear your voice. What is the word on the two agent's location?"

"Sir, they have just left the hotel after checking in to room ninety three. I believe they are going to William Legg's house, if that was correct."

"Great. Are you sure that is where they are at?"

"Yes, sir, I am sure. They asked me if he still lived in this town, and I said yes. At the same place, they asked, and I said yes. They should be back here tonight, though, if I was led correctly."

Monroe smiled. "Great."

23

Xavier froze. "What do you mean? You can't mean what I think you do, can you? You've actually found my father?" He looked around, sweeping Parker off of his shoulder. Raphael nodded nonchalantly. Xavier's eyes glinted with false hope, but Raphael soon wiped it away.

"As you already know, William was the first on the case after you and Joseph mysteriously disappeared. Well, after all of this time, he has a lead. But, despite that, something tells me you won't like it." Silence commanded him to go on. "Mr. Legg thinks that the same people that took you also took Joseph. So, in that case, your father just may be in the same place you came from," he said. "Like Nico said, the motive may as well be to use you as a weapon; but, in this case, without their two top resources, the United States stands in a weak and feeble state as of--" He would have continued on, but a phone rang in his pocket. Raphael looked around at all of the shocked faces staring at him before pulling it out. Within a few taps on the touch screen, the phone was unlocked.

"Hello?" Raphael held the phone up to his ear. A muffled voice that sounded worried came blasting from the phone's speaker. Immediately a horrified look crossed Raphael's face.

"Nicolas, is there a television around here? It's urgent." He threw the words out of his mouth as if they were poison. Nico nodded, confused, but then led him over to a room next to the kitchen. In it were a few couches, a bar with stools at it, and a flat screen television, which had on it a blank and black screen. Raphael raced over to the remote that was sat on a recliner's arm and swept it up into his hands.

Raphael slammed the power button on, causing the television to flash to life. After a few clicks of a button, the television was focused on a news channel, one that had a reporter inside of what seemed to be a reporting room. The female reporter had a look of panic, anxiety, and fear on her face as she leaned onto the desk she was sitting at.

"The United States of America is in a code-red panic state." The words froze Nico, Ally, Raphael, Derrin, and Xavier in their spots. If there were any words that the five did not want to hear, it was by far those.

"A code-red is about the worst thing that can happen to a country," Raphael explained to anybody that would listen, although he knew that everybody was aware of what a code-red was. In part, Xavier thought Raphael said it because it made *him* feel comforted. "It means something tremendously horrid has happened: there had never been a case of it happening since the precaution began in 2015. In a code-red, leaders of the most powerful countries are called together in an immediate meeting held in Washington, D.C. Although the public *was* ignorant to this meeting, they are all too aware of what the code means now. Through the years, though trying to be withheld by the government, the press and public have had ways of discovering what they needed and wanted to know about the emergency state. Finally, the government leaders of major countries decided to open up about the code-red policy. And, now, *this* happens."

The five adults in the room looked at each other, afraid of what they would hear next from the television. "President Robert W. Clemons has been taken hostage while at a vacationing home in South Alberta, New Mexico. Although this was his one, week-long vacation out of the entire year, it seems like trouble follows where his Secret Service does not. Police, SWAT, and Navy SEAL teams of all kinds and divisions have been called in to investigate. So far, police have released no information of any kind, and that includes any information of leads about the suspect. As of right now, one thing is certain; the country is in panic. Therefore, we recommend that all viewers and citizens of this country stay off of the roads, and if possible, people in all major cities need to stay inside at all times. We do not know what will happen next, but we want to be as safe as possible. Small towns are not instructed to do the same, but it will be a precaution that is almost impossible to not undertake in."

The worried expression on the newscaster's face

turned upwards into a false smile, though it fooled nobody. She was still scared, as any normal person should be.

Xavier stared at the television, wide-eyed. He couldn't believe that the president, the one whom he and his father were supposed to protect, was abducted. In a way, he felt that it was his fault. After all, it was his job to protect Clemons, wasn't it?

When he couldn't bear it anymore, Raphael turned the television off. He sat down, suddenly unable to stand. Derrin rubbed his hand over his face, a move that was becoming close to being dubbed his signature move. Parker sat down as well, almost to weak to breathe. Nico stood in his spot, his feet glued to the floor and his face frozen with horror and disbelief. Ally sat down, water coming to her eyes. The only one who seemed to be unaffected was Xavier. Of course, he felt guilty of this crime, but yet he didn't have any memory of knowing the president. Though he knew what this meant for the country, Xavier couldn't quite bring himself to feel sad, angry, or discouraged. All that mattered to him right now was finding Joseph.

Suddenly, a thought occurred to him. "Nico, you don't think that he could be the same place as my dad, do you?" Heads turned towards him, including Nico's.

"W-what?" He whispered in a stuttered response. Nico seemed to deny it before considering the idea. He stared off into space until Xavier's voice snapped him out of it.

"Nicolas!" Nico's head jerked up, waking him from his daydream.

"What? Oh, yes, I mean, I don't see why we couldn't consider it. But why would the- I mean, that place- do something as major as that?" Nico stumbled. Thoughts zoomed by Xavier's mind so fast he thought he could almost see them.

"You said Monroe, the boss, liked Clemons, right?" Xavier asked, turning to Parker. The guard looked at him and nodded, confused.

"Yeah, yeah, sure, he liked him well enough. It was those two other jerks that wanted him dead. Are you sure they didn't take him?" Simon brought up a valid point. *Why would Monroe take one of his friends hostage?* Xavier thought, obviously confused. There were simply too many variables in an experiment he did not want to be apart of.

24

Joseph Hider's eyes snapped open. They were wide with fear; the green and gold mix of his iris's gleamed as they looked around anxiously. Three people stood with their backs towards him, making him want to know who they were. Despite his tired state, Joseph could plainly make out the figures in the room around him.

A man dressed in a black suit was staring out the only window, and two large, bulky figures stood by the metal door, making six people in the room altogether. The man in the suit swung around and revealed himself to be the one person Joseph plainly hated: Martin Monroe. A smile rose on Monroe's face as he saw Joseph's eyes open.

"Good, Joseph, you're up!" Monroe said with fake but believable joy. Joseph rolled his eyes and wearily sat up. The bed he was on was not very comfortable, and the tiled floor did almost nothing to help his aching feet. His stomach grumbled, telling him obviously what he already knew: he hadn't eaten in over a day, and now he was starting to feel the major effects. An exploding headache crept over him slowly, tempting him to fall back into sleep and stay that way forever. Fire spread throughout his joints in which connected his shoulders to his body, and his hands to his arms. He thought that perhaps it was from the fighting he did before he was in this room, trying to escape from the guards. Although, he was still there, which meant that it did not work.

On the sill of the window sat a tray, one that held a glass of orange juice, two buttered bagels, and some sort of fruit that looked to be a mango. The view of just these objects made Joseph's mouth water and his stomach grumble even more.

"Oh, I'm sorry, are you hungry?" Monroe asked in a mocking tone. Joseph's upper lip twitched in annoyance. His stomach, on the other hand, answered Monroe with a hearty growl. The man in the suit only smiled, knowing that he had won.

"Bug off," Joseph growled through his teeth. Monroe only smiled once again. He motioned for the guards standing by the door to leave, and, after hesitating, they finally relented and left. Upon seeing the other guards leave, the three guards standing by Joseph's bed followed their peers and left.

"Listen here, Joseph. Your little friend, Robert Clemons? We have him here." The suited Monroe leaned in towards Joseph's face, a sign of dominance. Joseph's eyes only widened with disbelief and horror.

"No, no, you can't, that's a lie." He shook his head, refusing for it to be true. Robert was a good friend of his, one that he knew Monroe would use against him. Monroe already had Xavier, now he couldn't, wouldn't, let anything happen to Robert.

"Well, you better start believing and cooperating, buddy boy, because listen here. If you don't start telling us exactly what we need to know…" Monroe trailed off while staring menacingly into Joseph's eyes. "We can always get it out of you using Robert. I'm sure that his bloodcurdling screams would make you more than happy to comply. Do you understand?" Joseph's eyes widened even more, knowing that Monroe wasn't lying.

Martin Monroe got up and walked towards the door haughtily. His hand was on the knob before he looked back and smiled. "Think about it," he said with a wink. Hate flowed through Joseph's veins as Monroe stepped out of the door.

His mind started to dwindle towards his hatred until his stomach growled, reminding him of his situation. With a fleeting chance of hope, he looked over to see if the breakfast tray was still there. It was.

Joseph was immediately up and over by the window. He wasted no time in picking up the bagels and virtually shoving them into his mouth. The blueberries exploded into his mouth, followed by a big gulp of orange juice. His stomach was no longer drowned with hunger, although it would still take a lot more food to settle it. Joseph picked up the mango and bit into it, savoring every last burst of juice until the fruit was gone.

He looked out the window after downing the last of his orange juice. The endless Sahel desert gazed in on him like a lion watching its prey. The yellow-tinted sand waved miraculously in the wind, as though it was a picture coming to life. It reminded him of a movie he had just seen. In fact, it was the last movie he had seen in a while.

It had been just the two of them, Joseph and Xavier, going to the movies together to watch a R rated movie. Xavier was thrilled, because he was only fourteen at the time. It had been that long ago.

Thoughts of his son ran through Joseph's head. The memory he had held on to had been the one he was fondest of, one that he would be happy to live over and over everyday.

He and Xavier had been at a baseball game; it wasn't a major one, just a minor league team that eventually led up to the major league. The batter, the star player on the home team, had just hit a home run and the ball was flying in the air. Young Xavier anxiously held up his mitt, wanting to catch his first fly ball. With taller men surrounding them, Xavier had no shot of catching it if it even came his way. Of course, as Joseph couldn't take the heartbreak of his only child, he quickly swept Xavier up and sat him on his shoulders. The ball came flying in, landing in Xavier's mitt.

Saddened sighs came from the men around them, while Xavier pumped his fist in the air with excitement. Simultaneous laughter erupted from the pair as seven year Xavier jumped down from Joseph's shoulders.

Extreme sadness and disappointment drug Joseph from his memory. In his heart, he knew that Xavier was in the same building somewhere, probably being hurt or starved, or both. The worst part was that in no way could he deny that it was his fault. In truth, it was all his fault; he blamed himself. It was Joseph that got Xavier introduced into this work, and it was because of him that Xavier was here now, probably dying. No amount of physical torture could compare to what he suddenly felt in guilt and sorrow.

25

"We obviously need to do something about my father! We can't just stand around here bumbling around like fools! After all, this is what Nico, Parker and I came for!" Xavier said, making heads turn towards him. When nobody else spoke, he took another turn. "You said he was probably taken by Monroe, right?" Xavier turned to Raphael. "Well, if that's true, and that's a pretty big IF, we should probably return to Nico's village house, agreed?" For a moment, silence swept the room like a gust of wind in the Sahara. Then everybody started talking.

"I'm in!" Parker.

"We're not sure if he's even there!" Nico.

"What would we do even if we went?" Ally.

"I say we go for it." Derrin.

"If it's in the president's protection interest, and if it's the only lead we've got, I say go for it." Raphael.

All of this was said at once, making for a loud occurrence. They all seemed to be repeating what they had just said. Finally, after minutes of loud discussions, Nico stepped in.

"CUT IT OUT!" his loud voice rang out over all else's conversation. Everybody stopped talking and looked towards Nicolas, shocked.

"Look, we have no other lead, agreed?" Some nodded solemnly, wanting to hear what Nico had to say. "And just like Raphael said, if it's involving Robert's protection, then we should take the only chance we've got, yes?" Now everyone's head nodded, although some were slow to agree. Xavier could see the reason in this, but it seemed very far-fetched to him.

True, it was the only shot he had, but was it really worth going halfway across the world twice in one day for a guy he didn't even remember?

Xavier looked around curiously. Ally seemed deep in thought: she was staring out in space. The others, on the other hand, looked very concerned over what Nico had brought up. He guessed that it was the long flight that got them thinking, not the fact that they had to travel halfway around the world to save somebody who might not be there. Not complicated at all.

"How are we even going to get there?" Raphael asked. Heads turned towards him. It suddenly gave everybody a new thought to think about. Derrin had no idea, but the others were all thinking the same thing.

"Take my plane," Nico suggested. Now the heads turned towards him. The patrons of the room had seemed to forget that Nico had in fact all the money that he could need, therefore allowing him to have his own jet. Ally shrugged, allowing herself to give an introduction to what everybody was thinking.

"Let's go!"

Only two hours later, Derrin and Raphael had canceled their hotel reservations and were on their way to Nico's plane, along with the others. William had been told about Robert, but he claimed to already know from his own television in his study. Ally rolled her eyes, knowing that, that was a lie and he had in fact not known about Robert. Derrin smirked, enjoying his sister's annoyance. Until only a few years ago, he had known her to be the one with the best temperament out of the whole family. Now, Derrin and Ally shared the same opinion of their father, although not to the same extent.

"Um, guys," Derrin said when the companions were about ready to get on the plane; "I have to make a call." He held up his hand, motioning to his phone. Xavier looked at Parker, and Parker looked at Xavier. Xavier shrugged.

"Uh, okay, but hurry up." Xavier followed the others up the ramp and onto the plane. The plane hadn't been turned on yet, and Derrin was relieved that he would be able to talk in peace and not struggle to hear the other end. Quickly, as if he was trying to time it before the plane started, he punched in a few numbers on his touch-screen phone and then held it up to his ear.

Alex jumped as her phone rang loudly, snapping her out of her daze. She had been sitting at her desk, furiously typing her keyboard. In truth, Alex was deeply worried about her companions Derrin and Raphael. No one knew where they were, only that their last check-in was when they bought a flight ticket. Alex always worried when she wasn't in control: it was wired into her, she couldn't help it. It didn't help that her ex was the one she had to worry about, but she had no doubt that they were together. Rapahel would almost certainly look after Derrin with his life: in a way, they were brothers.

"Hello?" She rested her phone between her head and her shoulder, allowing her to continue typing. Silence greeted her moment before somebody finally spoke.

"A-A-lex?" Spark's head snapped up from her computer.

"Derrin! Where are you? Is Raphael okay? Why didn't you tell anybody you were going?" Alex bombarded Derrin with questions, making him smile. Now, though, the plane was just getting started up, the gigantic turbines throwing gusts of wind everywhere. This made it almost impossible to hear anything, but, regardless, Derrin knew what Alex would be saying.

"Alex!" Derrin had to raise his voice to be heard over the wind. "I can't exactly hear you, but listen close. You've heard about Robert, right? Of course you have. Well, Nicolas Hedge, Joseph's brother, thinks he has a lead. Get this, it's in Africa. I'll give you the coordinates, and I need you to get there as fast as you can. We can deal with the others later, okay?" His words came pouring out of his mouth, desperate to reach the phone before they were swept away by the wind. The door of the black bullet opened and Xavier stepped out and came running down the stairs towards him. His short, wavy hair was flapping along in the wind, making Derrin smirk.

"Listen, Alex, I've got to go," he said after giving her the coordinates. "Talk when you get there." Right after he finished his last word, Xavier arrived.

"Come on, you're going to miss the plane!" Derrin nodded his head and smirked, embarrassed.

"Oh, of course, sorry."

The pair jogged hurriedly onto the plane and shut the door behind them. Raphael caught Derrin's eye curiously. After years of knowing each other, Raphael had learned to tell when Derrin was nervous, scared, or had any emotion out of the ordinary. Immediately he questioned it.

"Derrin, who was that call to?" Raphael asked calmly, as if he already knew the answer. He lounged back in his seat, fumbling with a piece of string in his hands. Now everyone's attention turned towards Derrin.

Knowing that he had to make up an excuse and fast, he thought for a few seconds before responding.

"Somebody from the office called when I was at the hotel. I missed it, and they would worry and send somebody out to find us if they thought I was missing. I mean, I didn't tell them anything. I just said that we were off on a vacation. Together..." he trailed off as Raphael's head jerked up.

26

"Oh, come on, you know it wasn't that big of a mistake," Derrin smiled apologetically at Raphael while he sat in the chair closest to him. Sitting next to Raphael would hopefully take his mind off of flying, but not being able to see outside was a plus.

Xavier rolled his eyes as he set off into the cockpit where he greeted Nico and the pilot. The two seemed to be deep in discussion, so Xavier decided he had better not annoy them. *Better safe than sorry,* he thought. He turned to leave but then overheard the pilot speak.

"Are you sure Xavier, is, um, okay?"

"That's none of your concern. Your job is to fly the plane, not worry about the latest gossip. Got it?" Xavier squinted, trying to figure out why they were talking about him, but then realized that if Nico caught him, he would be supervised the entire plane ride. Xavier didn't want that.

Xavier plopped back into his seat. Above all things, he couldn't believe that he was going to go back to the place that started his memories, though it was the same place that took them away as well. Oh, the things he would do once he got his hands on the person who did that to him. Though, he supposed he really couldn't do so, however much he wanted to. He had no idea of what they looked like, so how could he ensure that he got the right person?

William had gotten onto the plane, but he was alone sitting in the corner. Xavier stared at him. *Why is he always alone?* he thought. The answer wouldn't quite come to him, but he figured that it was the only peace he would get away from his family and the drama. After all, wasn't William one of the two people that helped them make it that far?

Eventually, drowsiness swept over Xavier, although he didn't feel any hint of tiredness before he got on the plane. Xavier supposed that it was the calmness of the room that soothed him although the lights seemd to be becoming less dim as minutes passed The comfortable seats greeted him, wiping away his problems until the serenity was so great he couldn't resist sleep.

At first, he slept calmly; it was only after an hour that dreams and memories overtook him.

———

Xavier jerked up, his whole body doused in sweat. He was pulled back against the wall, latching his back and the wall together. Xavier's breathing became faster and faster as he realized with rising horror what this memory was.

A look at his surroundings told him that he was back in the Org., the one place he definitely did *not* want to be. The room was not unlike the size of the one he woke up in last time, although it seemed smaller because of the medical machines scattered along the room. A metallic beeping clicked every other second, drawing his attention. It was one that reminded him of a heart monitor.

As he was forced to stare at what little he could see of his area and what bleakness he could see of the ceiling, a person stepped over him and into view. What was plainly a female stepped farther towards him, revealing a pale face with dark black eyes staring at him with a grim smile. The white lab coat suggested what Xavier already knew.

"Hello, Xavier. I'll be your doctor for today." The same devilish smile washed over the doctor's face, causing Xavier to grimace. From a table right next to the one used for operation, the doctor picked up a scalpel and a pair of surgery scissors. Xavier's eyes widened as he imagined all of the things that could be done to him.

"Now, X, here's how things are going to work between you and me. I'll just do this real quick, you might feel a little pinch, and I'm done. No struggling, okay? It is something I very much do not want to deal with today." When Xavier didn't reply except for a snide raise of his upper right lip, the doctor proceeded on. "Okay, I'll take that as an okay. Now, you'll feel just a little, or maybe a major-" the doctor laughed, "prick. Don't worry." She took the scissors and glided them across Xavier's cheek, only making Xavier breathe faster with fright.

The doctor pulled on white, latex gloves and snapped them over her wrists. "This will only hurt a little..." she trailed off as she grabbed the scissors and proceeded towards Xavier's head with them. He let out a blood curling scream, hoping that anybody would save him from whatever was about to happen. But if anybody heard him, they certainly didn't come to his rescue.

Xavier jerked up once again, only this time he was laying down on a couch on Nico's plane. He sighed with relief as he saw Parker sitting right next to him. He put his hand to his forehead, and only felt a thin layer of sweat. A glance over at Parker confirmed that everything was normal: he seemed to be lost in space as an audio book blared through his headphones.

Nicolas was nowhere to be found, so Xavier assumed that the cockpit was where he was. He groaned as he sat up, still expecting to be sore as he was in the dream. His head hurt, but Xavier assumed that it was caused from the recent rising of the plane into midair. It always hurt his head when that happened: it seemed as though he never remembered to chew a piece of chewing gum while they rose and landed. It, technically, was Parker's job as Xavier's best friend to send out a friendly reminder, though Xavier granted him that he was asleep as they rose into the blue skies.

Xavier looked over at Parker and slapped his shoulder. Parker's head turned, giving Xavier his attention. After pulling out his left ear bud out of his ear, Parker asked what it was that he wanted.

"Parker, how much longer until we get there? How long have I been asleep?" Knowing that it had taken them two hours to get to Independence, Xavier had concluded that it would take roughly the same amount to get back.

"You've been asleep for roughly an hour and a half. We should be actually passing through Chad right now… I don't know, check out your window." Xavier sat up fully against the window and rubbed his head wearily. He realized that there was in fact a piece of plastic with a small indent in it, indicating that it was put there for a reason. When he pulled it back, a circular window appeared. With interest, he looked out. Bleak yellow desert stared back at him. Occasionally, a small little, green dot would intrude on the bleakness, making Xavier think back to the village. It wasn't quite a village like the one Nico had a house in, but rather, it was an oasis. Soon, though, in a matter of seconds, the little green dot was gone from view. Only then did Xavier let it sink in how much he was completely surrounded. Not by people, though; he was surrounded by the endless deserts of the Sahel and Sahara. Sure enough, he could take a dune buggy and hope to reach a village like Nico's, but who knew how long it would take to reach one, and the luck it would require? Of course, he had no intention of making a run for it, but if the situation required it, what would he do? Xavier stared off into the yellow desert while he thought.

After being caught in silence with his thoughts, Xavier saw Nico enter the room from the front, holding a platter of delicious looking entrees, including biscuits, muffins, pastries, and fruit. Xavier's attention was grabbed by the scrumptious-looking food as he looked towards Nico, who was setting the tray on the coffee table. When nobody spoke up, obviously mesmerized by the food, Nico spoke.

"Well, if it helps, these should be eaten *only* when landing. Which will be in about twenty minutes. So, if you do, which you probably will, eat these before, be sure to leave some for the descent." Xavier smiled and nodded, reminding himself to keep this note in his mind. He did not want a sore head when they got to Nico's house. He would certainly need all of his brain that he could use to get his father back.

"Xavier, I have something to tell you," Parker said as he leaned over close to Xavier's ear. Xavier raised his eyebrows in question.

Parker's voice came out as a whisper. "Xavier, while you were sleeping, we made a plan. A plan, I mean, of what we're going to do once we get to Nico's house." Xavier immediately sat up straight, anxious to hear more.

"Well, I've got to go back to the *place*," he spat out the last word, "alone. Without anybody, that is. Then, after I can successfully be sure of getting Joseph and Mr. Clemons back, I will send a signal to you guys, who will be right outside of the building. Then, we'll get in, get them, and get out. After that, we'll-" he was cut off by Xavier.

"What, you made this all *without* me? How? Why? No, I won't let you go in there alone, it's not happening!" Xavier said with as much force as he could without letting the others hear. Parker only shook his head.

"Xavier, I'm sorry, but you don't have much of a choice. Look, I know your opinion is very important, but this is the only safe way. I promise, I'll be okay. You'll see," he said with a confidence-boosting smile that Xavier didn't quite believe.

27

It was only a half an hour after Nico brought out the food that the bullet landed behind his house. By that time, the passengers of the jet were more than anxious to exit the plane and get onto stable ground. The food, as it had turned out, was actually an object that helped make everyone's descent a little more pleasant than it had been the other time. Despite the food, though, Xavier actually tried to drift off into sleep before they landed, but flashbacks of his dream taunted him. There was definitely no way he was going to risk having another horrid memory hit him like the way his previous one had, especially if he concluded what happened right after his last memory.

After giving it some deep thought, Xavier had decided to tell Nicolas and Parker about his dream. The reasoning behind this came from the fact that those two were the first ones he told about his memories, and they may be the only ones able to help. Sure, William or Raphael might know something, but he preferred to keep it between himself, Parker, and Nico. The only problem was going to be getting them alone. Now, that they were all in the desert, close to the *one* place, they would all certainly have things to discuss with everybody. In a way, that created a problem. It wasn't that Xavier didn't want anybody to share their ideas: he did. But getting Nico and Parker alone, together, would present a problem. There was a slight chance that nobody would notice their absences; after all, they were among the four most important people in that house at the moment, or so Xavier had thought.

When all of the luggage (which wasn't much) was loaded into the house, Nico's pilot took the jet and flew off. Xavier didn't question where to: he had more important things on his mind. He wasn't even thinking about where everybody would stay, how much food they had, or how long they would be staying in the desert. His mind was focused on their plan.

It was only a few hours after they landed did telling Nico and Parker about his dream sound like a bad idea. *They already have enough on their plate right now, don't they? Maybe I can tell them after everything…*

28

"Monroe will almost definitely have Robert there," Nico said dreadfully. As much as he wanted to be oblivious to the truth, he knew there was no hiding it. Joseph and Robert were almost surely at the same place Xavier had been those days ago, but who knew what was happening to them? *My own father may not even know who I am,* Xavier thought. *Then again, I didn't even remember his face until I had that flashback.*

Thoughts ran through everyone's heads. Most of them were worried about Joseph, but William was mainly focused on Robert. *After all, the president is much more important than a replaceable agent, even if he is director of America's most valuable agency. Isn't he? Robert, he is the president! Doesn't he deserve my thoughts and worries more so than Joseph?* It wasn't a question of divided friendship; rather, it was an ultimatum of loyalty. If he had to choose between one of them, well, how could he choose?

"We can leave tomorrow, if there's no convincing you all otherwise," Nico spoke again after everyone had agreed on going. If they could even find Joseph, Xavier had no problem going back to that place. After all, wasn't that what he was trained to do, save people?

Dusk was beginning to peak over the rising dunes, sending drowsiness upon everyone in the village. Ally yawned and brought up the topic of sleeping arrangements. Since there were seven people all in a three bedroom house, two people had to take the couches on either side of the waterfall. That left Derrin and Ally on the couches, Xavier and Nico in their rooms, and Raphael sleeping on the floor of the guest room with Parker. William had walked out of the house, telling everyone that he would find a place. Nobody believed him, but then again, nobody stopped him. He wasn't seen again that day.

This was the first time Xavier had even thought about sleeping after the plane ride. What a flashback he had had there, he did not want another one following suit of it.

Xavier entered the same room he had slept in

before. It looked fairly the same, and of course it did. Nobody had gotten the chance to enter it after he had left it. He flipped off the light switch and the room became dark, the sun just leaving his room. The patient unrolled his thin blanket and sheet and slid under them. After deciding that having a memory was a risk he had to take, Xavier let sleep overtake him.

At first, he slept peacefully in the dark, but then a faint memory came upon him.

Xavier opened his eyes. He could hear his heartbeat racing as he looked around. He could tell that the same room he occupied was obviously the same one that his last memory came from, but yet this time it was different. No doctor, no knives to cut him with, nothing. Oddly enough, he seemed to have no trouble sitting, which was what he was doing, or breathing, which seemed like a good sign. The metal bench Xavier was sitting on was not uncomfortable, but his head hurt. For one thing, he was sweating profusely. That he knew. The patient could feel it condensing on his forehead until one small drop fell onto his hand. He was convinced it was sweat until he himself saw it. When Xavier looked at his lap-laden hand, he saw the drop was red. Blood red.

He jerked his head up from where it rested on the wall. When the patient turned around to look the wall, it had blood molded in the shape of his head on it. A quick gasp escaped his mouth as he stared bluntly at the wall. *How could so much blood come from my head? Except...* he didn't want to think about finishing that sentence.

This memory, despite his worries, was right after the surgery. Immediately right after it. He tried to remember anything, but he couldn't. That's how he knew. No words popped out at him, no objects brought the heavenly glow he had learned to call memory. Nothing except the recognition of the room felt similar to his last flashback.

Xavier gingerly put a hand up to the back of his head. The blood was sticky, leading him to believe that the surgery was at least half an hour ago. He didn't know for sure, though; it hurt to think deeply.

A knock came from the metal door, followed right after by the same door being pushed open. A male figure walked in. the person was dressed in a doctor's coat, not unlike that of the operator. Not that he remembered, anyway.

In the person's hand, a needle shined brightly alit in the dim light. It was almost if the light wanted Xavier to know that the needle was for him. As the male approached, the needle seemed more and more dangerous.

Xavier just sat on the metal bench as the figure came and stood in front of him. Then, the supposed doctor held out his hand, as though he was expecting something from Xavier. Xavier froze. Although the doctor was wearing a face mask over his mouth, he could hear it when his breathing quickened.

When Xavier didn't put anything in his hand, the doctor rolled his eyes. He grabbed Xavier's elbow and held it up. Xavier flinched, but he figured a needle couldn't hurt too much. He didn't protest when the needle was injected; instead, he took the time to scope out the young male and decide if he was a threat or not.

The doctor was a male, of that much Xavier was sure. At a closer look, he saw the brass nameplate attached to the doctor's coat. "Jay Williams," the nameplate read. Xavier took this as an advantage.

"Jay," he said, his voice croaking from the lack of use. Jay looked down at Xavier's face but then back to his arm as he took the needle out. After not saying anything back, the doctor took off his mask. He sighed before speaking.

"What? I'm not supposed to be talking to you, and if I were you, which I'm glad I'm not, you had better make it quick," Jay muttered while pulling out a stopwatch from his pocket. He clicked the top, his eyes moving from Xavier to the watch. The patient's eyes began to grow heavy, and all of a sudden, a rush of drowsiness overtook him. Still, he needed to have answers.

"W-w-where..." was all he got out before he sank into sleep again. Jay clicked the stopwatch.

Xavier's eyes jolted open and he jolted up in his bed. His breathing was fast as he wiped sweat off of his head; this time, he drearily hoped it wasn't actual blood. When he saw it on his hand, it confirmed his hopes.

His mind raced back to whatever he could call it. *Well, what was that about*? A thought came to his mind, one that pointed out similarities in his recent memories. In his first dreams, he had actually been an observer, not himself. That was a start to decoding the meaning behind these. Still, questions flooded his mind. Why did his mind replay these dreams? Why did they happen almost every time he slept? Nico had said that Xavier's first two out-of-body experiences were probably caused by stress, his mind being too over exhausted to relive the entire memory. It didn't quite make total sense to him, but it was the only reasoning he had, and he had to go with it.

Xavier stole a glance at the clock, which read 6:30 AM. *Why is it always me that is up early?* He thought, regretting deeply not persevering through the dream longer. Figuring that he had no chance of going to sleep, Xavier stood up to stretch. He didn't hear anyone in the kitchen, but he didn't want to be the first one out there. The only way he could think of passing the time was searching around the room to see what he could find, so he took to that. He didn't expect to find anything, but it was the only way to pass time.

29

Nico opened his eyes wearily. His alarm clock blared on his night desk, screeching "wake up!" at him every chance it got. The small robot-looking clock flashed light into his room as he groaned.

He rolled over onto his left side and slammed his hand onto the alarm. When that didn't quiet it, he picked it up and examined it. Still half asleep, Nico was unable to make an accurate diagnosis, so to get rid of it, he brought his arm above his head, clock in hand, and then threw it across the room. It flew in the air, still screaming. When it reached the wall, the alarm hit it and fell to the ground, silent. Nico smiled.

"Goodnight," he muttered before succumbing to sleep.

Five minutes later, the clock sputtered loudly from across the room. Nico groaned when he realized that the alarm clock was battery powered and it wouldn't stop beeping after being unplugged, which was what he was counting on. Slowly and angrily, Nico got up and trudged over to the wall opposite of his bed. When he found the alarm, he ripped off the bottom lid and tore the batteries out. He made a mental note to never put them back in.

A yawn escaped from Nico's mouth as he looked at the clock on his wall. Even though he had an alarm clock, he always needed to be sure of the correct time. When he realized that it was 6:45 in the morning, he figured it was time to start breakfast. *Better make it before Parker gets out there,* he thought to himself haughtily.

Even though he was tired, Nico pulled a loose t-shirt over his tank top and opened his door. The room was dark, and the soothing sound of the water fall made him want to sink into sleep again. He looked over to Derrin and Ally on either sides of the waterfall. They were both fast asleep, which meant that he had to be extra quiet when preparing breakfast. He looked over to the kitchen, and a figure was already sitting at the bar. Although he was still half asleep, he could see that it had the sleek formation of a woman; also. because she had long hair and a small figure, her gender was easily recognizable.

"What the.." he whispered to himself as he double checked Ally on the couch. She was still there, sleeping soundly.

"Who's there?" Nico asked as he approached the figure. The person at the bar turned, and Nico froze when he saw her.

Alex Mansur turned around to face the shocked Nicolas. She smiled sleekly as he recognized her. "Why, hello Nicolas. How have you been?"

Xavier could hear two people speaking, even over the slashing of the waterfall. He wasn't too tired anymore, so he decided to meet the people out there. That, and the fact that he was beginning to get hungry persuaded him.

Xavier opened the door and shut it quietly behind him. The room was dark, but the light overhanging the kitchen was on. Raphael and Derrin, though, were still asleep on the couches. That left Xavier wondering who could be at the kitchen, since there were two figures.

As he walked closer, clearly one had their back to him. The other was Nico, who was standing on the opposite side of the island.

"Good morning Nico," he said. Nico smiled, but it was almost if the smile was rehearsed and not natural. The other person turned around, and he then got a look at their face. It was a female, of course, but this one brought back memories. And those memories weren't good.

Immediately Xavier started backing away slowly. "Nico, what is she doing here? Wait, who is *she*? Nicolas, I know her from somewhere, I'm sure of it!" he demanded answers of his friend. Xavier couldn't place her, but he knew that she was an enemy, spy, or something, whether it was secret or not. The girl only smiled devilishly.

"That's no way to great your boss, is it now, Xavier?" Xavier froze. He might not like her, but boss? Where was this coming from? Suddenly, a realization popped into his head. He announced it just so loudly as to not wake Derrin and Ally as he approached her quickly.

"You're Alex, aren't you?" He said it more as a statement than a question. Once again, the girl smiled.

"Clever boy now aren't we? How do you remember? If I've been caught up correctly, Nico here tells me that you've gone and got your brain wiped." Another grin, like she knew something he didn't. Instantly Xavier rolled his eyes, making sure that Alex didn't think she was in charge of him just that easily.

Nico finally spoke up, making sure that Xavier didn't get so mad as to get close to blows. "Xavier, she's right. Well, and yes, you're right too. But tell me, how did you know? Did you recover anything else?" Now, Nico was almost frantic with happiness folded with excitement. It was the chance of Xavier recovering any of his memory that really got Nico going; but what could he say, he worried about the kid.

Xavier looked oddly at Nico. "What? No, of course not! Don't you think I would know it if my memory started coming back?" Xavier spat out before instantly feeling horrible about yelling at him. Nico stayed quiet, but Alex broke the silence.

"Oh no, not this again. Xavier, you always were quite a complainer, don't you think so Nico?" She turned to Nicolas who was dumbstruck, jaw hanging open wide. Xavier walked furiously up to Alex, and he would have given her a piece of his mind if Nico hadn't stepped around the island and in between the two. Xavier furiously stomped off to a seat around the island as far away as Alex as possible. She just smiled. Xavier looked away to ignore smacking her.

To change the subject, Xavier brought up the subject of which was the reason he came into the kitchen so early. "So, Nico, what's for breakfast?" Nico, who was facing away from Xavier and was cooking something on the stove top, just turned around and smiled a warm, hearty smile.

30

Parker and Raphael had both woken up and were seated at the island in the kitchen. Raphael was the first one to awaken after Xavier, followed closely behind by Parker.. Derrin was still asleep when Raphael got up and walked into the kitchen. He stopped cold when he saw Alex. Confusion crossed his face, but then it was instantly replaced by accusation.

"You followed us? This is a new low, even for you!" Raphael shouted as loudly as he could without waking the sleeping Ally and Derrin. This time, Alex didn't smile, she only looked away. Nico looked towards her, a new point brought up.

"Wait, how did you know where I live? You've never been here before," he said, anxious to know the answer. The people who were awake looked towards her in an accusing manner. She only looked around at everyone, and then to Raphael.

"Is it your job to know? And no, Raphael, I did not follow you." It was said quietly; she was obviously trying to regain her sense of control over the room. When nobody looked away from her, she tried a different approach. Alex sighed before talking again. "Derrin told me," she said, truly sounding defeated. Now the heads turned towards Derrin, who was asleep on the couch. As if almost on cue, the agent rolled over onto his stomach, snored and continued on sleeping. Raphael rolled his eyes.

"No, no way. There's no way that he told you. Anyway, if he would have, he couldn't. He had no chance to. He didn't even make any calls, except for.." Raphael trailed off , his face dropping as he remembered the call. Alex smiled, knowing she at least had won that statement.

"No..." Raphael muttered to himself, almost so quiet that nobody but himself could make out the words. He looked over at Derrin and rolled his eyes once more. Alex responded.

"Now, Raphael, you don't really think I would lie to you, do you?" She smiled, making Xavier's stomach turn with something similar to hatred.

"You really want me to answer that? After what we've been through?" Raphael replied. Alex's smiled dropped from her face.

"Perhaps not," she said, looking towards Nico. His back was turned from everyone; it sounded like he was scrambling eggs or doing something of the same sort on the oven top. The tension was high in the room, higher than when the news spread about Robert being taken.

Ally woke up and walked over to join the crowd at the island. She said the smell of bacon woke her up, but then she changed topics and asked who Alex was. When nobody answered, she moved on to yet a different topic.

"How are Parker and sleepy head over there still sleeping?" Ally asked while taking a chair and sitting in it. She motioned to Parker when she said "sleepy head." Xavier shook his head: it really wasn't a topic he wanted to talk about. Right now he just wanted breakfast and peace. Nico ducked down and took out a bag from the cupboard below the sink. Xavier just passed it off as flour or sugar, but when the smell of freshly brewed coffee hit his nose, he wanted more.

"Nico, is that coffee I smell?" He hadn't had any drink other than pop and water since he woke up, and his taste buds ached for something more. Xavier had a feeling coffee would suit them perfectly.

Nico turned his head around and smiled. "It is, glad you remember at least one heavenly object. Would you like a cup?" Xavier anxiously nodded his head at Nico's offer.

A cup was set in front of Xavier, and steaming hot liquid was poured into it. The smell was in fact heavenly, like Nico had said it would be. The first drink burnt the tip of Xavier's tongue, but then he got smarter and drank it in little sips. He still had his eyes on Alex, who was talking quietly to Raphael, but since the other agent seemed to trust her, he figured he should too. But Xavier couldn't override the feeling of anger and uneasiness when he was around her. Something in his gut commanded him to get away from her, or to strike at her, either one, but he had to fight it. The way he saw it, Derrin wouldn't have called her if it wasn't for the best. *Right?*

At the stroke of noon, all were awake and ready to embark on their journey. William still hadn't returned, but Derrin had made the others agree to go on without him. Alex was beginning to get caught up on all of the latest actions, and she brought up the statement that Robert was more important than Joseph, so therefore they needed to get Robert back first. Xavier instantly declined, stating that it was his father that brought the country's protection up from nothing. The others just stood back and watched as the two butted heads.

Eventually, though, after too many minutes of arguing, Xavier stopped talking to Alex and walked away from her. She took it as a win for her, but Xavier refused to accept defeat. Right then, however, Xavier decided that his main focus should be getting his father and Robert back.

The crew was dressed normally, with the exception of Parker. He had his uniform that he brought back from the Org., and he intended to use it.

The plan went like this, as Xavier would explain it to Ally after she asked to be caught up. The faint memory hit him, informing him that he in fact didn't remember Ally being with the others while they made the plan. "Parker will go into the Organization and beg Monroe for his job back. Then the others will park land rovers outside the perimeters of the building, behind a big sand dune. It will be impossible for anybody involved with the enemy to see, making it vital in our plan. After Parker discovers where Robert and Joseph were being held, he will drive to the others, letting them know it was time. Then, the team will barge in and try to get Robert and Joseph safely. It was as simple as that," he told her.

"Why was I not told about this before?" Ally demanded angrily. Xavier just shrugged, "Um, that was Nicolas's job? Besides, why didn't you help make it while we were on the plane?" He ended it as a question because of the uncertainty in his voice. Ally shrugged in response. "There's really nothing to worry about," Xavier continued as the team went out the back door of Nico's house.

Four dune buggies greeted them kindly. They were all a light tan, one that blended in perfectly with the sand. Xavier stared that them blankly, shocked.

"Nico, how?" he asked, smiling. "Where did these come from?" Nico only walked up to his side and smiled.

"Xavier, stop doubting me. I have my ways. Now, are we going to go or are we just going to stare at these beauties all day?"

31

Xavier and Nico rode in the first buggy, followed by Derrin and Ally, Alex and Raphael, and Parker by himself in the last one. Xavier let Nico drive, because he supposedly knew the way. It wasn't like Xavier didn't, though, he just did not want a repeat of what happened the last time he rode over the dunes. If a flashback happened while he was driving, he and Nico were both in danger. Having Nico drive was an easy solution.

"Good point," Nico said after Xavier told him his reasoning behind not driving. He turned back to face the other companions, who were all sitting down and strapping their seatbelts. The wind was nonexistent, so Xavier gladly didn't have to yell himself hoarse trying to talk to the others.

"Okay, listen up!" Nico started out. To project his voice more, he stood up. Nico started quietly laughing when he saw this. Xavier turned and faced Nico.

"What is so funny?" he asked, expecting a smart and sarcastic answer. Nico pulled Xavier's arm down, telling him to sit down. He reached into his own pocket and pulled out a thin metal slate. The front was glass, and Xavier instantly knew what it was. Stupidity washed over him. Nico, happy at his own genius, laughed some more. Nico pushed a button on the side and the glass lit up. He pressed a button, held it up to his ear, and started talking. Xavier rolled his eyes.

"Or you could do it that way," he muttered. Xavier's own pocket vibrated, reminding him of his own speaker. He pulled it out, turned it on, and listened to what Nico had to say.

"You all remember the plan right? Well, if you don't, ask your neighbor. It's not that hard, people. Now, the question arises. Are you all ready?" Nico spoke to the other drivers and riders. A series of yes's and a few sure's came back, signaling that it was truly time to go.

"Good. Follow me and try to keep your engine noise level down, okay?" The same answer replied, and Nico lowered his goggles to his eyes. Xavier did the same, and then they were ready. Nico pressed his foot down, instantly getting a response. The buggy lurched forward and then they were off.

The parade circled to the side of Nico's house and then turned onto the gravel path leading through the middle of the town. Dirt flew back from the first dune buggy's tires, making splotches of dirt dot over Derrin and Ally's windshield. This, in effect, happened to every other dune buggy following them. Parker was especially glad that these dune buggies had windshields, as a comparison to the one he had last ridden. Though, they were prepared for this; the windshields and goggles helped them, even though the sand still blotched every buggy except the first one. Nico smiled when he looked back and saw what he had created.

32

The parade arrived behind an enormous dune within the hour. Nico pulled up, and Derrin, Raphael, and Parker came up beside him. Nico pulled out his phone and started talking with Xavier listening intently.

"Okay, Parker, you go ahead. Phone us when you're getting ready to come out, okay?" Parker nodded, seemingly excited to go ahead and get his job done. Parker took a long look at everybody before reversing his dune buggy and then driving around the dune, out of sight.

Though he didn't show it, Parker was nervous. His breathing was fast and his eyes darted back and forth between the building looming ahead of him and the phone in his pocket. The Organization, as Xavier called it, also Parker's old workplace, grew bigger and bigger with each passing minute. The plan loomed ominously in his head. *It's foolproof,* he thought to himself. *Okay, maybe it's not...But it is too late to turn back.*

He arrived at the door of the Caplar, the building he had once ran away from. One glance back saw him a yellow desert with hills of sand rolling across the horizon. There was no way anybody would be able to spot the rest of the crew.

Parker took a deep breath before getting out of the buggy and walking up the large hangar door. On the small, indented wall beside it, a keypad rested, waiting to have somebody punch in the code. He hesitated, hoping that the code wasn't changed after Xavier's escape. If it was, he had no other plan, and then what would happen? After sighing, Simon flipped up the key pad flap and rested his finger on the number one

"One, zero, one, nine, five," he muttered to himself while typing it in. Before typing in the five, he paused. Simon sighed once again before typing in the last digit.

The keypad beeped two times before the hangar door *whooshed* open. Relief flooded into the guard, and the knot in his stomach untwisted. He exhaled before climbing back into the buggy and driving into the Caplar. After he was in, the hangar door dropped down behind him.

The Caplar was the same inside as it was the last time he was in it, although the same buggy he was driving was missing from it's spot. Parker drove in carefully, trying to keep the vehicle as quiet as possible. He wanted to get in, get his job back, and get out. In his mind, it wasn't a sure fire plan, but it would have to do.

After parking the vehicle and walking into the hallway, he shut the door quietly behind him. A hum came from the ceiling, announcing the airway's presence. Flashbacks of meeting Xavier in the bathroom came flying at him, but he decided to focus on his task and worry later. Parker looked up and sighed before striding through the hall. A few rights and a left brought him to a wooden door with two windows beside it. The windows, though, didn't show the hot desert outside; it gave way to Martin Monroe's office. Without being noticed, though, he slowly peeked his head out of the corner of the window, stealing a glance at the office behind it.

The same wooden desk with the same motionless person sat in the room, all alone. The man was Monroe, there was no doubt about it. He had the same emotionless look on his face as he did the last time Parker encountered him. Simon hated that look with sincerity.

With sheer determination and a mediocre bit of fear, the guard stepped in view of the window and towards the door. Monroe didn't notice; he was too busy typing furiously on his laptop. Simon knocked twice on the door, hoping to get a sliver of Monroe's attention.

"Come in," Monroe muttered, his attention not leaving his computer screen. Parker turned the knob and entered the office.

"Sir?" Parker asked quietly. He knew that he had to make it believable that Xavier took him; in return, that started with giving Monroe the respect he demanded.

The manager looked up, startled by the guard's voice. His face fell with disbelief when he saw the producer of it.

“Simon? Is that really you?” Monroe whispered. He stood up and walked over to the guard. “Where have you been? Is X with you?”

Parker sighed heavily, rising and dropping his shoulders. “Look, I've come to get my job back. X, the patient, he forced me to help him, he threatened to kill me if I didn't. But I've escaped, and now I'm here again. I-I don’t know, really, what all happened, but will you accept my help?”

Monroe stood, dumbstruck. “I, well, of course you can come back. Just out of curiosity, is there any chance you know where the patient is?” His lips curved to one side in hope of the right answer, the one he wanted.

Simon looked down at the floor and slowly rocked back and forth from his heels to the pads of his feet. In his head he was angry that the second thing he asked about was the patient, but his face didn‘t show it.

“Sorry, sir, but he didn't let me see. I had a sack over my head the entire time, and I mean that quite literally." He looked back up, meeting Monroe's eyes. "After I told him what direction to go, after he forced me to, that *scum* dropped me off in the middle of the desert. Mind you, he stole one of the buggies, so that's how X made his escape so lively." Parker looked back at the floor and shuffled his hands behind his back. "I did manage, however, to catch a name. Yours, in fact. I don't know, sir, how he remembers, but one thing is for sure: he does. He remembers every little detail that he did before he arrived, sir, and he's angry."

Through Parker's whole speech, Monroe stood, speechless. The room was silent, Monroe's mouth slightly agape in disbelief. Seconds passed before Monroe straitened his posture and flattened his tie. He coughed slightly before returning to his desk silently.

"Good, Parker. Go back to your office and then return to your post. I'll visit you later to see how you've adjusted." Although he was back at his desk, Monroe didn't immediately start typing. He just stared out the window, seeming to be in thought.

"Yes, sir." Parker went to exit the room before Monroe stopped him again.

"Wait, Parker. There are some new files, they document everything that you might have missed. We've got a project, and I've decided to let you know about our most recent one before that." Monroe smiled as he spoke. Parker just nodded and exited the room.

Parker let out a big sigh as he walked down the hall towards his office. Sweat covered his brow, threatening to give away his secret. Although nobody was in the hallway, he couldn't let anybody discover his lying ways, so he wiped the sweat off of his brow with the back of his hand and hurried to his office.

33

Simon sank into his chair and rested his head against the back of the chair. The padded seat, back, and arm rests invited him to stay there forever, and the guard was tempted to, but he had work to do.

Groaning, Simon sat up and leaned forward. On the wooden desk was a rectangular slab with a red top on it. It rose a centimeter from the desk, and so Parker assumed he knew what it was and opened it. A white screen popped up at him and keys were on the lower side of that. His eyes scanned determinedly across the screen, his finger running across the computer, controlling the mouse on the screen. Files upon files opened before he finally found the ones he wanted. "President," "Hider1," and "Hider2" appeared on his screen, stealing his interest away from the others.

"Hmm," he hummed while looking over the first link. He snuck a quick glance at the door and window into the hallway to make sure they were closed. After deciding that they were closed and nobody would see in, Parker clicked on "President."

A range of photographs, articles and notes popped out at him. Piece after piece filled the small screen, each one of them demanding the guard's attention. When the last photograph appeared, Parker decided that it was time to start looking through them. At first it was nothing he didn't know; pictures of Robert, fragments of his latest speech, things of that sort. But towards the end of the pile came the interesting things. A picture of a handwritten note on yellow paper popped up onto the screen, dotting his interest. His jaw dropped open when he read it. It seemed to be an unknown person's handwriting, that he was almost positive on. But then, after he studied it, he seemed to vaguely recognize it as one of his fellow guard's.

"Date: Tenth of June, 2098. Our plan is now officially set. You know of it, don't you? Have you forgotten? After all, it is in your state of mind to not remember things of this such importance. Clemons, does that ring a bell? Of course it does. If it doesn't, I don't want you on this After the stage of amnesia, Clemons will then agree with us to defeat the forces of his country. Then, after as much as many months have passed, we will take control of the remaining countries on this

planet. Nothing will stop us, do you think not so as well? Together, we will take control of the world, and nothing will stop us! I've taken the risk of getting Monroe to agree to this, and he has firmly agreed to help us, therefore strengthening our allies. After all, is this organization not with the purpose of the same thing? The people of other places, they are beneath us! Why should we have to bow down to them when they are so much less than us?"

The one patient, Xavier, as they call him, seems to be of great importance. I have heard the word that he worked for the government; they called him a 'protector of Clemons.' Do you know what that must mean? If not, it means that Joseph and Xavier must know each other, therefore it will be of greater chance that they remember! However, they both have the last name of Hider…do you think they are related? What if they remember? It is not that I do doubt the surgery procedures of Baron, but these worries do grow on me. What do you think?

If it is possible, return a note to me as soon as possible. I find that, even though we are busy, notes are the most efficient way of talking, aside from a face-to-face confrontation. Please give your return note to Anthony so he may deliver it quickly.

Sincerest well wishes,

Bryien."

Parker's jaw was dropped open as far as it could be.

Disbelief not only flooded his mind, but his entire body as well.

"No way," Parker murmured in awe as he closed the letter. *Just wait until Nico and Xavier get a hold of this,* he thought anxiously. After scanning through the rest of the files and making sure nothing was important, he saved the letter to his own computer chip.

A computer chip, as it was universally known, was an almost microscopic chip used to save important data. Every worker at the Org. had one specialized for them, making it easy to access information on their computers. His own computer chip could hold up to 700,000 files, far more than any hard drive ever could. The guards all carried their own specially programmed chip, but Parker made his own very unique in a way the others' weren't. His own computer chip could painlessly be injected into his own hand, in the skin right before the wrist. When it was in his hand, he had access to every single bit of information on the chip. The micro-programmed artificial cells bonded with his own, and in a way he didn't know, his brain had the knowledge of the chip. It almost seemed too impossible to him, but Parker didn't argue with it. It worked, and that was all that mattered.

"Okay, let's see what else you contain," Parker said to himself while clicking on "Hider1." Once again, information covered the screen in scanned pieces of paper, photographs, and newspaper. New yet valuable information was saved onto Parker's chip, strengthening his hopes.

He clicked onto "Hider2," assuming that it was Xavier's file. It was, giving him a glimpse of exotic hope once more. More pictures of his friend popped up, and then articles from newspapers appeared. Of course, none titled his kidnapping; if the American public didn't even know of Xavier's existence, how could they report of his disappearance? *They can't*, Parker thought in response to his own question.

"President Clemons; secret head of security is headed" was the closest anybody outside of the organization had gotten to realizing Xavier's existence. That, and, of course, his family's friends and all who knew him through family relations. They had sworn to secrecy, though; it had thankfully taken at least some pressure of off Xavier's shoulders while he guarded the president.

Parker smiled at the article. He remembered it quite well; it had thrown the CPAA off guard, and not in the slightest, either. Precautions had to be taken in order to ensure Xavier's protection from society. Although the certain newspaper company was not aching for money, it had to file for bankruptcy the morning after the article on Xavier was printed. Nobody knew why, not even some of the workers. Some said it was a miracle, for they had been reporting false information for years, but then others saw the true meaning of it. Those particular few had to be otherwise convinced that it was just the president's friend who was visiting from elsewhere, not a mysteriously trained killer who was the son of the CPAA's coordinator.

Although the newspaper article was interesting to read again, it was another piece of information that caught Parker's eye most of all. He was just beginning to delve deep into the details when a hoard of loud sirens and flashing lights suddenly came on. Parker looked around, quickly jumped out of his chair, and bolted to his door. Once he had it open, he stepped outside. He looked to his left, but he couldn't see anything. He looked to his right, and stopped. A guard was quickly running towards him.

34

"David," Parker shouted over the noise, relieved to see somebody that he didn't hate. David said Parker's name and nodded at Parker, acknowledging him.

"What is this all about?" Parker asked, trying to regain composure. He couldn't avoid the feeling of hope that a member of his team was there, but in truth, he didn't want that. That just meant more troubles for him to deal with, and that was something he already had enough of.

"Sir, it's Project X. He's come back, and he's inside of the Caplar as of this moment. No guard is in there, we've waiting for your command. Although, I took the liberty of calling my team of five others here; they should arrive soon." Parker nodded, his mind secretly reeling. *Why is Xavier here? What does he think he's doing?* Parker's brain struggled to process the questions, but he motioned for David to open the Caplar door. Behind him, though, he could hear the five other guards arriving.

David opened the Caplar door and followed Parker in. The other five followed closely behind. Parker took note that they weren't armed; however, they looked quite dangerous. Even though none of them were the head guards, and some were thin and wiry, five against two were not good odds.

Parker anxiously glanced around the hangar. Then he saw it. Right in the middle of the Caplar stood the escaped patient, Xavier Hider. He had his hands on his hips and was staring at the door, as if he was expecting just this. Parker had to bite his tongue to hold back a smile of relief. Xavier was okay, but anger boiled in

Parker. Hadn't they enforced a plan? Oh was he going to kill Xavier once they got out of there.

Simon Parker, how nice it is to see you. How have you been, since, you know, you abandoned me? I've got to say, that was the highlight of my day." Xavier sarcastically smiled, and Parker's heart sank for a second before he remembered that the others did not know of the pair's previous adventures. This is all a show, he had to remind himself. He doesn't hate you, not actually.

Simon hurried to devise a plan of what to say to Xavier without giving anything at all away. Finally, he came up with a comeback. "I wouldn't be so sure of that, Xavier, when, after all, you were the one who took me against my will and forced me to help you. Oh, and, by the way, my day or two in the desert was spent nicely, thanks."

Xavier sarcastically smiled once again. "I would not be too sure about that, Simon. I did leave you the buggy, or do you not remember?"

Parker frowned, putting on his best angered face as he could. If he had to stand in front of all of these guards who would easily kill him, he had to make his hatred for Xavier at least believable. Parker turned to David and rolled his eyes.

"No, strangely, I do not remember that part. I remember you dropping me off in the desert with a bag over my head and telling me to leave. David," he turned to his co-workers, "take this *peasant* to Monroe's office. I'm sure, that, since the sirens and red lights don't reach the other end of the building, that he will be quite oblivious to what has happened."

35

Parker walked in front of the other six people as they ventured further and further towards Monroe's office. In his head, Parker's newly devised plan swirled throughout his brain. Questions flew everywhere, threatening to escape out of his mouth. *Will this work? What happens if we can't do it?* This was no time for doubts, though; his self-made plan had to work, and in order for that to happen, he had to let Xavier know of it.

The leading guard stopped in the middle of the hallway, motioning for others to do so as well. He jerked his head to the left, walking a few steps further away from the group as David approached.

"David, don't you think Xavier, is, um.." he trailed

off before looking up and meeting David's eyes. An evil look spread across Parker's face, and for a second, David realized the truth. But before he could say anything, Parker was in action.

Simon high-kicked David's stomach, making him stutter back until he hit the wall. The other guard hunched over, writhing in pain. After getting out of their shock, the other guards rushed towards Parker. Even the two holding Xavier forgot their duty and rushed to Parker. Smiling in anticipation, Xavier rushed towards the two and pulled them back by their necks. His grip was excruciating, making the two guards yelp in pain. Easily, he pushed them to the ground on their stomachs. Before they could react, Xavier pressed an instant pressure point on their neck, almost effortlessly knocking them out.

Meanwhile, Parker dealt with the three other guards. Two of them pinned the struggling Parker against the wall by his shoulders while the other one punched his chest. Parker groaned in pain while the other hit his stomach. When the one hitting his stomach pulled back to gain momentum, Simon took his chance. Using the two holding his shoulders as momentum, he threw his legs up and out, his feet colliding with the oncoming guard. In return, the guard sank onto the floor, clutching his stomach.

Xavier ran over to a guard who was holding one of Parker's arms and easily knocked him to the ground with two sickening punches, a kick, and one uppercut to the jaw. While that was happening, Parker slammed the other guard's head against the wall, easily knocking him out.

The sirens weren't blaring, the lights weren't blinking, the hallway was silent. Xavier smiled at Parker before speaking.

"Good plan, Parker. I'm shocked. Actually, no, I'm not, not really. Well, anyway, what's next?" He came up to Simon and patted him on the back. Xavier looked around the hallway.

"I remember this. My room was, um, that way," he pointed straight as he said it. Simon smiled slightly and nodded.

"Yes, it was. And it just so happens that we have to go that way." Simon made a move to start walking, but then Xavier stopped him.

"Parker, listen to me." The guard turned and looked at him inquisitively. Xavier continued. "Look, the others are still out there, and they are waiting for the signal. They know I'm in here, but they still think they are coming in. But, Parker, I came alone for a reason. If we come across someone or something we can't handle, I don't want them getting hurt. I can't let that happen." He looked down sadly before Simon patted him on his back.

"I understand, Xavier, you don't have to explain."

Xavier looked up and nodded. "You're right. Let's go."

A few turns, a metal door, and one conversation later, Simon and Xavier arrived at Xavier's old door, which happened to be where Joseph was just moved.

Parker was too preoccupied with his own thoughts to try and decode what Xavier was thinking. *Why was I just told of the files? Was it true that they were just created? Why did Monroe keep Hider1 and President from me? Does he suspect something?*

"Parker!" The returned guard jerked up at the mention of his name. Xavier was staring at him, an odd look on his face. "Sorry to wake you up from Simon Land, but we somewhat need the key for the door." Parker snapped himself fully back into reality and nodded.

"Oh, right, yes." He pulled out a key ring he had obtained from his desk and picked out a certain key.

Testing it, Simon put it into the lock and turned. The lock clicked, signaling success. The pair looked at each other before opening the door. Xavier nodded and Simon opened the door.

Inside, with his back facing them, a tall but muscled man stood with his hand behind his back. The suit he was wearing was torn and tattered, but his posture suggested a not-yet-broken spirit. At the sound of the door opening, he turned stealthily and looked. His face was crossed with emotion and shock as he saw who was standing in the doorway.

"Xavier?" Joseph questioned. Xavier's face was still as he slowly stepped towards his father. Joseph quickly closed the gap between them and pulled his son into a tight hug and closed his eyes.

"Xavier, I can't believe it's you. They told me you escaped, but, but, I didn't know what happened. Are you okay? Are you hurt?" He pulled Xavier back and put his hand on his son's shoulders. Joseph looked from Xavier's feet to his head, making sure he was okay.

"Father, I'm fine, really, I promise. But there are bigger things then you and me right now. The president, Robert Clemons, is here, and they want to do terrible things to him. The same things they did to me..." Xavier trailed off sadly. Joseph's face transformed from happiness and shock to realization.

"Son, what did they do to you?" His voice was quiet now; quiet and full of compassion. Xavier just shook his head and looked back up.

"That's not important right now. What is important, on the other hand, is that we get Robert to safety." He turned back to Parker, who was standing in the doorway and staring at the floor. "Parker, do you know where Clemons is?"

The guard's head jerked up once more. "What? Oh, yes, I think I do." He smiled before exiting the doorway, motioning for the other two to follow. Joseph and Xavier shared a shrug and then hurried off after Parker.

36

Eventually, the threesome arrived in front of a door similar to the one they had just exited. Once again, Parker pulled out a key and repeated the same motion as he did with Joseph's door. The metal slab opened, and it revealed the president of the United States.

At first fear crossed over Robert's face, but then recognition appeared. "Robert! Xavier! I'm so glad you are here! I've been so scared and worried-" He was cut off when Parker entered the room. Fear once again entered Robert's face.

"Stay away from me! That's a guard! He's wearing the same uniform! Get him away from me!" The president backed against the far wall, trembling with something so similar to fear. Parker walked forward with his hands held out in peace, but Xavier stopped him and walked up to Robert.

"Robert, this is our friend, Parker. He's helped get me out, and now he's going to help you. But in order for him to do that, you have to trust him. Is that clear?" Xavier asked. Robert looked between Parker and Joseph and hesitated before nodding.

"Yes, just tell me what I need to do." Parker smiled at Joseph's convincing attitude. Xavier looked back at Parker for instructions.

"You two need to get back to the buggies we have. There, a few of our friends and people you know are waiting there for us. Nicolas, Joseph's brother, is there, along with Alex Mansur and agents Raphael Sandriel and Derrin Legg." Robert's head perked up when he heard the familiar names. Joseph, on the other hand, objected.

"What? No! Of course I will not leave you two! I

just got my son back, and now you expect me to leave him? How will I know that he will be okay? No, I will stay and help you," Joseph said with forceful determination. Xavier sighed and walked up to his father.

"Joseph-" he started, but then thought better of it and began a new sentence. "I know this is hard, but we need you to do this. Parker and I, we have to do this on our own, do you understand? It is crucial at this point, and we can't afford anybody to go with us. Please, just do this one thing for me," Xavier said in a quiet tone. Understanding crossed Joseph's face.

Even though he was reluctant to do it, Joseph finally agreed. "Just point us in the right direction." Xavier smiled, and Parker and told the president and his guard how to get to the others and the buggies. Before the pair went, though, Xavier stopped his father.

"When you get there, be sure to tell the others not to come after us. We'll be fine. Are you capable of that?" Xavier stopped and looked at his father. Joseph nodded and then headed down the hallway with Robert in tow without looking back.

Parker sighed. "We've got to get to Monroe. He is the leader around here, if I haven't told you before. He will have answers." He started walking before

Xavier grabbed Parker's shoulder, commanding him to stop. Xavier's eyes were narrowed and his eyebrows were down, an inquisitive look.

"Parker, what's up?" Parker stopped in his footsteps turned around fully to face Xavier.

"I'm sorry, what do you mean?" he asked quietly. The same look stayed on Xavier's face.

"I know you've been acting different, you've discovered something, haven't you? Something bad, I can tell. What is it?" Parker froze. *How did he figure out so fast? Is it really that obvious?* He sighed, knowing that Xavier knew he was right. Simon was too tired to argue with Xavier, and with his determined nature, Simon knew Xavier would not give up until he knew.

"Xavier, I can't tell you how sorry I am..." he trailed off. Xavier's head jerked up in surprise.

"What do you mean? Why are you sorry? What happened? What do you have to be sorry about?" Simon just stared at the floor as Xavier asked the questions, while tears welled up in his eyes.

"Xavier," it barely came out as a whisper. "When they operated on you, you almost awoke during the surgery. They gave you a drug, a drug that made you sleep. It was brand new, it had never been tried. But later, after you left, yesterday, in fact, they tested it on a cat. Just some random cat." A single solitary tear ran out of Parker's eye and plopped onto the floor. "Xavier, that cat died." He looked up at Xavier's face.

Xavier's face froze, realization smothering him. "No, you're not implying what I think you are, are you?" His voice now was a whisper. Parker just nodded his head and looked down at the floor.

"I'm so sorry," the whisper came out of Parker's mouth before he continued. "The cat died instantly, which I thought would mean you had a chance, but I was wrong. I read more on your file that the drug, it's eating you from the inside out. Have you been able to hear your heartbeat loudly lately? That is a sign of it, they think. Xavier, I can't even begin to tell you..." he trailed off even more, his eyes now red. Xavier only smiled humorlessly and put his hand on Parker's shoulder.

"Parker, it's okay. We can worry about that later, but now we have to get answers, okay? Maybe, once we get out of here, we can find a doctor. Maybe somebody will be able to save me, okay? Just focus on this, and then we can worry about me." Parker looked up at Xavier. His bravery in this moment was unbelievable, or at least Parker thought it was. Though, Xavier was also right. There were more important things to do. Parker nodded and wiped his eyes on his sleeve.

"You're right," he said, sniffling. "I suppose we had better get answers first. After all, that's what we came here for, right? Answers, I mean?" A light smile crossed Parker's face, making Xavier all the more confident. He, and the pair started their inevitable walk towards Monroe.

In just a short minute, Simon and Xavier turned a corner and stopped. However unexpectedly, just twenty feet in front of them stood Ashley Baron and Martin Monroe, the leaders of the project that ruined Xavier's life. Hatred was smothered heavily on both of their faces as the pair stared at Xavier and Parker.

Monroe was leaning against a wall, and right beside him was Ashley, the one who performed Xavier's surgery. Xavier knew this, and, in a way, Parker figured it out from not just the look they shared, but the heinous look on Xavier's face.

"Well," Monroe said. "Look what the cat dragged in. Oh, sorry," he stopped. "I guess the cat didn't drag anything in, because the cat is *dead*."

37

Xavier just rolled his eyes, and yet he wondered how Monroe knew that Parker had told him. "That drug wouldn't kill me. It won't if it hasn't already," he spat at the person directly across from him. "And yes, I know about it." Ashley moved to the middle of the hallway beside Monroe and folded her arms across her chest. Doing the same, Parker tried to intimidate her. Much to his surprise, she merely humored him with a smile and a more upright position.

Xavier continued on while Monroe listened intently. "You think you have a hand on me, don't you? I can tell by the air around you that you think you do. Well, I am NOT a puppet of yours!" His voice continually got louder as his words went on. Anger broiled up to a point that Xavier had no emotion apart from that of hatred towards the two in front of him. Suddenly, Ashley and Monroe's face became more hardened, the smallest bit of realization quickly crossing them. Before Parker could recognize it as that certain emotion, the pair straightened up and regained composure.

"Of course you're not, Xavier. You never were. Just tell me one thing, just one. How do you remember? Do you remember everything?" Ashley asked. Monroe turned to her.

"What did you do wrong? You imbecile, you

cannot do anything right!" His voice was full of anger towards his partner, who just rolled her eyes.

"He cannot remember, or are you too stupid to realize that I've told you this already?" Ashley rolled her eyes as she looked over at Xavier. "You filthy liar, you remember nothing of your old life. Martin, you fool, you've been tricked!" Her last words were pronounced individually, each with hatred, loathing, and disgust.

Monroe looked quickly over at Xavier.

"Is this true?" Ashley did the same, only she rolled her eyes once more. The girl took the liberty of answering Monroe's question for him.

"Of course it's true, did you not hear what I just said?" she asked with a bite in her words.

"Quiet!" Monroe yelled at her; Ashley reluctantly backed down from his challenge. Meanwhile, Parker and Xavier were watching alertly.

"Yes, I do remember," Xavier whispered while looking towards Ashley and Monroe. Monroe stopped yelling at Ashley and slowly looked over at Xavier.

"You do?" His words were quiet, but they were not gentle. Anger and suspicion were held highly in his voice as he looked between Parker and Xavier.

"He remembers, why is that not enough for you? I can see it in your eyes, Martin. That will never be enough for you! What else do you want from him?" Simon yelled, making Xavier jump. He didn't expect the sudden, loud noise from his companion. Xavier looked over at the steaming Parker, who had steam coming out of his ears. His hand secretly moved from fists at his sides to beneath the lower part of the back of his jacket. Xavier looked closely and he found that he could see a rise in the pocket of the uniform beneath Parker's jacket. The guard's hand clasped onto the rise, and then Xavier could firmly see what it was. A gun protruded from the uniform Parker wore.

Careful not to draw attention to it, Xavier looked back at Monroe and Ashley, who had clearly not seen the gun. Monroe's shocked eyes met Xavier's, and his frown turned into a wicked grin.

"Xavier, you may not know this, but you are not the only person we need. Sure, it would help if you didn't remember anything, but we have reserve options. You know, Joseph, your little ol' father? Yes, Xavier, we have him. And you know what?" Monroe's smile turned into a move of intimidation, as Parker had tried, but only this time it spread a thin coat of fear over Xavier's anger. "We did the same surgery on him as we did on you." Ashley looked towards Monroe, confused, but then she caught onto his plan and looked towards the others and nodded in confirmation.

"Only, with him, he was awake the whole time. Every single cut, every single needle, every single knife and blade that cut his brain, he felt. He felt it all! I could hear his screams all the way from the other end of the building. In fact, he almost died. But we gave him a few shots, and, bam!, he was good."

Xavier's eyes widened as he imagined the picture Monroe was trying to paint. "No, no. Stop. You didn't do that. NO!" The last sentence was quietly but angrily said. But rejection kept bubbling in his voice, and by the time he got to the last word, he was almost screaming. Monroe flinched almost invisibly, but it didn't go unnoticed by Xavier, who lowered his voice.

"No, you didn't do that, you couldn't have..." he trailed off, his voice quiet. Monroe only nodded, as if confirming the fact.

"Yes, Xavier I did. And trust me, he felt. Every. Single. Cut." The wicked smile came upon Monroe's face again, making Xavier's stomach knot up all the more.

"No," Xavier muttered.

"Yes!" Monroe yelled, thinking that he had won.

"No!" Xavier's voce was louder this time.

"Yes, Xavier, he screamed out in pain for hours upon end. You better believe it, because it happened!

Xavier's blood was boiling at the highest temperature that it could be now. "NO!" he yelled at the loudest pitch he had ever yelled. Monroe smiled, and then Ashley froze. Xavier had pulled the gun from Parker's pocket and was now aiming it at Monroe. The leader of the Organization's face fell, but he didn't have time to duck. Xavier's finger was pulled back, and so was the trigger.

A bullet fired from the gun, producing an echo louder than Xavier's scream. It rocketed towards Monroe and arrived at the center of his chest, right beside his heart. It pierced through the first three quarters of his body and then carved its way through the rest of his chest. Monroe's mouth dropped open in shock, but nothing came out. He looked down at the hole in his chest, which was covered by his hands. When he revealed his hands, they were drenched in blood.

Monroe fell to the floor, hitting it with a thud. Ashley reacted first, leaping over to his body and kneeling down by his side. Parker stared at the two, mouth hanging open in shock. Xavier had to pull him back into reality.

Xavier dropped the gun and turned to Parker. Grabbing him by the jacket, Xavier shouted one word: "Run!"

38

Xavier and Parker sprinted down halls, turning left and right countless times. Xavier began to get confused about what direction they were headed in when they arrived at the Caplar door. Parker reached his hand into his right pocket and produced a key ring. After fumbling for the right key, Simon finally inserted the key into the door and opened it. As soon as Xavier and himself were in, he slammed the door shut.

Already have been through this, Xavier knew the drill. He quickly ran over the door and waited for Parker to catch up. He looked at a dune buggy, and sprinted over to get inside of it. He rapidly pressed the button that turned it on, but when it did nothing, he moaned and then hopped off. Xavier ran quickly to the hangar door, their only option left.

When Simon got there, he ran over to the side of the door and slammed his hand onto a red button.

Almost immediately, the door started rising, giving Xavier his cue to slip under it and start his trek. Parker followed him, not bothering to close the door. What mattered now was escaping.

"The team is just over that hill! Let's call them!" Xavier panted, trying to motivate himself as well as Parker. He reached inside of his pocket and swore when he realized his mistake. *My phone must have fallen out of my pocket when we were running,* he thought, laying the responsibly on his companion.

"Parker, do you have your phone?" he asked. Parker stopped, looked at him, and frowned.

"Xavier, it's at my desk inside! Oh well, we don't have time to go back. We have to get over that hill!" Xavier's feet sank into the sand each step, making it impossible to go any gait faster than a slow walk. *At this rate,* Xavier thought, *we'll be there in ten minutes: too long!* Although, Parker lagged a few steps behind, already out of breath.

Xavier was five feet ahead of Parker and almost at the base of the hill when he heard it. A gunshot pierced the air, ruling over every sound he heard. He froze, making sure that he wasn't hit. Much to his relief, he was okay. Xavier thought then that the bullet probably missed him, and he was right. But when he looked back,

Xavier discovered that he had just witnessed the one moment he wished he was wrong.

Parker was hunched over, his hands clutching his stomach.

"No," Xavier whispered as he looked for the source of the bullet. His eyes searched the desert until he saw, at the door of the Caplar, Ashley Baron was holding her gun up, aimed at him. Xavier kneeled down on his knees next to Parker, who was on his back, writhing in pain. A groan escaped his mouth, but Xavier's eyes were locked on Ashley.

The surgeon went to pull her trigger again, but the gun just clicked. She checked the gun once again, and cursed when she realized she had just used the last bullet. Quickly, she ran inside the Caplar.

Xavier looked down at Parker's stomach, only to realize that the bullet had pierced his stomach and blood was leaking out of the hole. Parker's mouth was opening and closing, almost if he was trying to speak.

Tears were starting to come out of Xavier's eyes as he tried to get Parker to speak.

"Simon, no, Simon, no, no, no, no, please. Don't do this," he stuttered while meeting Parker's eyes. The young guard smiled lightly, although Xavier knew it hurt him to do anything.

"X-Xavier," Parker whispered in a stutter. Xavier acknowledged this by nodding. Parker only smiled again. "You have to," Parker stopped. "You have to leave." At this point, every word hurt Parker more than the last, but he had to get this out.

"No, Parker, I'll take you with me. I'll go and get the buggies, then we will come back and bring you to Nicolas's house. Then, we'll, we'll, we'll take you to a doctor, or a surgeon, or-" he was cut off by Parker, who pointed out the guards rapidly approaching.

"There's no time. By the time you yell and get the buggies over here, the guards will be upon us, and both of us will be of no use. Besides, I will weigh down the both of us. Xavier, do this for me, you've got to go. Now!" The last word was blurted out. Xavier stood up still looking at Parker, tears streaming out of his eyes.

"No, no, I can't leave you..." He trailed off while staring at the guards. Parker only got Xavier's attention by yelling one word.

"Run!"

Xavier could barely see out of his eyes, but he knew

Parker was serious and right. The guards, even though they were on foot, were somehow running through the sand and approaching very quickly. One doubtful look down at Parker confirmed his thought. Carrying Parker would no doubt weigh them both down into the sand, making it impossible to get away. Parker mouthed the word "Run!" once more before jerking his head towards the hill.

"Parker, I'll be back, I will, I'll be back!" Xavier said before rocketing towards the buggies. Even though it was almost impossible to run without sand shoes like the guards had, Xavier forced himself to travel as fast as he could up the hill. Knowing that it would only cost him time, Xavier forced himself to not look back. He couldn't afford it now.

Once he got to the top of the hill, his team caught on and drove up to him. Nico pulled up to him, and Xavier jumped into the front seat. One last, fateful look back caused him to see Parker, only this time he was surrounded by guards.

"Parker, oh no, Parker," Xavier whispered out of hearing range of anybody else. Nico pulled up to the top of the hill and froze.

"Xavier, is that Parker?" Nico asked, although he said it more as a statement. His emotionless voice hurt

Xavier all the more; though, his best friend had just died, and he thought nothing could hurt him any more than he already was. Disregarding the pain momentarily, he managed a quiet "yes" and a nod to answer Nico.

"He told me to leave him. Parker had a point, though. If we went back for him, there is no chance that we could fight off those guards." Xavier pointed out, but then insanity took over him as he panicked. "No, no, wait. Nico, we have to go back! Turn it around! Nicolas, we have to go back now!" Hysteria was setting in on his voice.

"Xavier," Nico said, grabbing his attention. "Xavier, I'm sorry, but we can't go back now. If we did, we would only get more people hurt or even killed."

Xavier's mouth was wide open as he looked away from Nico, eager to hide his tears. "We have to, I promised him." He looked at Nico, his voice quieting. "I can't break that promise."

Nico only shook his head. "Xavier, I'm sorry, but we have to go." With that being said, Nico quickly pressed the gas pedal down, pulling Xavier's line of sight down the hill and away from Parker.

"No, no…" Xavier seemed to be collecting his

thoughts once more as his indecisive feelings took over again. "Nicolas, no, we have to go back!" Xavier screamed, taking his voice from a whisper to a yell as he made a move to jump off. Nicolas only grabbed his shoulder and pulled him into the seat, forcing him to stay seated.

"I'm sorry," he said without slowing down. "Let's go," Nico told the others over his phone. Without saying anything else, they pressed their accelerators and drove off towards his house. With slight hesitation, Derrin looked back at Parker and the guards before following Nicolas.

39

After a little while, the team was back at Nico's house, and this time they had two new adults with them. Although Xavier had earlier anticipated that the house would be noisy, it was dead silent. He didn't want to deal with anyone, though; he went inside of the house and sped off to Nico's room. He would have went into Parker's room, but there was no way he could afford to do that.

Xavier slammed the door behind him and fell onto Nicolas's bed. It wasn't that he didn't want to see his father: he did. He just needed to be alone right now.

Xavier let out a deep sigh before letting the tears come rolling out. He cried for his father, who had to endure fear and pain throughout his stay at the Organization. He cried for his best friend, Parker. Parker, who had been the one to help him escape the horrid place, the one who understood him the most, his best friend. His best friend that was now dead, and all of the fault fell onto Xavier's shoulders.

Parker's last moments were relived in Xavier's head. *I left him. How could I do that? Why didn't I carry him? I could've picked him up, and he would still be alive right now!* Anger boiled up to the top of his skin. Tears rolled down his cheek and plummeted onto the blanket of Nicolas's bed.

The alarm clock roared, snapping him out of his trance and angering him all the more. Xavier wanted to be all alone with his thoughts and no interruptions, and the alarm clock had ruined that. He angrily clasped his hand around the clock, brought it behind his head, and threw it against the wall with extreme force. He didn't watch it, but he could hear it shatter into many different pieces. Xavier would have smiled if he wasn't heartbroken.

It's all my fault, Simon died because of me. I killed him, and I let Joseph get taken. And the president, too. He felt like the world was crumbling down on him, and it was all directed onto his shoulders. Xavier put his fists onto his forehead, trying to hide the tears from any imaginary person in the room.

Look at the bright side, a voice in the very back of his head said. *Joseph and Robert are saved, and nobody else got hurt. Except for William, maybe.* Now, Xavier's stray thoughts wondered back to the old man. *What happened to him? Why hasn't he come back?* Though, to be honest, he didn't really care about William. That man, he was invincible. He could take care of himself. *He left us, though! He doesn't deserve my thoughts,* Xavier mused harshly, though he decided to shove it out of his mind.

A before-unnoticed telephone rang on the bedside table, making Xavier open his eyes slowly. He sat up wearily.

The telephone kept ringing, demanding Xavier's attention. He reached for the phone, fumbling it before holding it up to his ear.

"What?" he yelled slightly, expecting it to be somebody from the kitchen. Instead, it was a voice he thought he would never hear again.

"Xavier," the young man's voice on the other side of the phone said ferociously. Xavier squinted his eyes in confusion.

"Parker?"

THANKS!

-The first is God, because without Him, I'd be nowhere. Then, I have to thank my beloved parents for at least letting me attempt to write a book. Without their support, I wouldn't be writing this. Thanks to my language teacher, Mrs. Heller, who was one of the people who have helped me immensely in writing this. After all, she is the one who created the assignment that turned out to be this book. Also, I can't forget to thank the rest of my family, who were delighted to find that I was writing a book. And to my friends, who were mostly excited about me writing a book. Thanks to Derrin Ireland and Stephanie Mansur, who let me use part of their names to craft the most diverse of characters. Finally, thanks to anybody that reads this, whether I know you, or you are a total stranger from halfway around the world. Every reader is as equally important!

ABOUT THE AUTHOR

Madison Jackson is an avid enthusiast of Thoroughbred horse racing, tennis, and obsessively writing short stories or poems of all genres. She has eagerly loves the black racehorse Decisive Moment, and she even managed to pet him once or twice. The inspiration for *The X Variable* came from a three-paragraph essay for a Literature class focused on description. Her essay turned out to be the rough draft of the first chapter in the book. *The X Variable* is her first book.

Made in the USA
Charleston, SC
15 October 2013